Faster than the Rest
MacLarens of Fire Mountain

SHIRLEEN DAVIES

Book Two in the MacLarens of Fire Mountain Series

Avalanche Ranch Press, LLC
PO Box 12618
Prescott, AZ 86304

ISBN-10: 0989677311
ISBN-13: 978-0-9896773-1-8
Library of Congress Control Number: 2013948249

Cover artwork by idrewdesign.

Description

Handsome, ruthless, young U.S. Marshal Jamie MacLaren had lost everything—his parents, his family connections, and his childhood sweetheart—but he's back in Fire Mountain and ready for another chance. Just as he successfully reconnects with his family and starts to rebuild his life, he gets the unexpected and unwanted assignment of rescuing the woman who broke his heart.

Beautiful, wealthy Victoria Wicklin chose money and power over love, but is now fighting for her life—or is she? Who has she become in the seven years since she left Fire Mountain to take up her life in San Francisco? Is she really as innocent as she says?

Marshal MacLaren struggles to learn the truth and do his job, but the past and present lead him in different directions as his heart and brain wage battle. Is Victoria a victim or a villain? Is life offering him another chance, or just another heartbreak?

As Jamie and Victoria struggle to uncover past secrets and come to grips with their shared passion, another danger arises. A life-altering danger that is out of their control and threatens to destroy any chance for a shared future.

Dedication

This book is dedicated to our two younger sons, Eric and Drew. Eric for his continued encouragement of my writing during this next chapter of my life, and Drew for being my web and SEO guru. Love you both.

Acknowledgements

I want to thank my editor, Regge Episale, who continues to be a patient guide through the writing process. Thanks also to my beta readers. Their input and suggestions are always welcome.

Faster

than the Rest

Faster than the Rest

Prologue

"Stop right there, Wicklin." The man's voice came out of nowhere, hard and unwavering. It was well past midnight in the deserted wharf area of San Francisco, a time when people could disappear without a trace.

Hamilton Wicklin stopped in his tracks and tried to make out the features of the man who stood in front of him. He was about Wicklin's size and dressed in similar fashion, which indicated he came from wealth. The voice wasn't familiar. *Do I know him?* He forced himself to stay calm. "Who are you? Are we acquainted?"

The man moved closer, moonlight illuminating a small pistol. "No, you and I are not acquainted, but I believe you knew my brother. Knew him well, from what I've learned."

"Your brother? Who is your brother?" Hamilton's mind raced.

"Was, Wicklin. He's dead. Died by his own hand after a poker game in which you were involved. In fact, you were the big winner that night. And the grand prize? The deed to my brother's warehouse, inventory, and accounts. You remember Jonathon Bellows, don't you?" The last came out as a sneer, the hatred evident.

"You're Bellow's brother? I heard he had no kin." Wicklin started to back away. He now understood the seriousness of this confrontation. Of course he remembered Bellows. Drunk, loud, and confrontational. It had only taken a few tricks, a few quick hands, and Wicklin had walked away with everything the fool owned.

"Stay right where you are, Wicklin. We both know you used your skills to fleece my brother. Others had you figured out, but my brother was drunk and didn't see it coming." The gun ground into Hamilton's gut, forcing him back against the edge of the waterfront. "Now, empty your pockets. We'll walk back to your office and pick up the deed to my brother's property. Then I'll decide what to do with you."

Hamilton handed the man his watch, money, and some loose tokens from his pocket.

"Well, well. What have we here?" The man used his free hand to pull open Hamilton's lapel. "I'll take those papers in your pocket, too."

Hamilton cared little about the watch and money, but he had hoped the man hadn't spotted the documents he had taken from his safe in preparation for a meeting with his attorney. Too bad he hadn't left them until morning. He handed them over.

Bellow's brother never took his eyes off Wicklin as he pocketed the papers. "Now, move." The man grabbed Wicklin's shoulder and shoved him.

A voice with a Mexican accent came from behind the two men. "Ah, señor, I see you have done my work for me."

Fear raised the hair on Hamilton's neck as he stared wild-eyed at Miguel Hagan, a murderous viper he had hoped to never see again. *How did he find me?* This was worse—much worse.

"Who the hell are you?" Bellow's brother hissed, and turned to point his gun in the direction of the voice.

One moment Wicklin's captor was threatening him with a gun, and the next he lay dead on the boardwalk. Miguel casually kicked the dead man's body over the edge and into the cold, turbulent waters of the San Francisco Bay, then pointed his gun at Wicklin.

Hamilton struggled to sound controlled, but his voice betrayed him, coming out in a choked whisper. "Miguel? What are you doing here?"

Miguel smiled. "It is good, my friend, to know you have not forgotten me, as I am sure you know I have not forgotten you."

"Uh, look, I don't have the money to pay you back. It's gone." Wicklin racked his mind for answers. He knew this man would kill him without regret, then walk away as if nothing had happened. Miguel Hagan was a cold-blooded killer.

"But you are a wealthy man, señor. Do not lie to me. You already cheated me of many dollars, and now I want them back. Your wife will suffer if you do not pay me." Miguel's words were calm but the menace behind them was not lost on Hamilton.

"You don't understand. My money, all of it, is locked up in a trust. I have no access to it. There's simply no money to give you." Wicklin was pleading now, begging for a life he realized he had already lost.

Miguel digested the words before he slammed his weapon into Hamilton's face. The impact broke Wicklin's nose and cut his brow.

Hamilton crumbled to the ground, grabbed his face with one hand and held up the other to ward off another blow. "Miguel, please. This won't get you the money you want."

"I fear you have had your chances, my friend," Miguel answered. His booted foot connected with Wicklin's stomach. "Besides, your wife, she has no love for you. She will be pleased with you gone."

The next strike broke Hamilton's ribs. He heaved and coughed. The last connected with his head. He writhed in pain.

"No one will miss you, my friend. You chose to cheat the wrong man. It is too bad for you, I think."

Hamilton didn't even feel the last blow before the cold waters of the bay swirled around and sucked him under.

Chapter One

"Talk to me, Tankard, or so help me God, I'll shoot you where you sit." Marshal Jamie MacLaren had reached the end of his patience. The lawman had followed Billy Tankard for weeks, sure the outlaw held the last piece of information Jamie needed to locate the hostage he had tracked for four long months.

Billy raised his head, a sneer twisting his tight lips. "I ain't telling you noth'n, MacLaren. Besides, you're a lawman. You won't shoot me."

"You think not?" Jamie's anger rose and he worked hard to keep it under control before he did shoot this piece of cow dung. "Maybe I left my conscience behind when I took on the job of finding the woman you helped kidnap." Tankard's eyes snapped to Jamie's, but he still said nothing. "Now, give me what I need or you'll surely wish you had."

Sweat beaded on Billy's forehead, trickled into his eyes. He swiped the moisture with the sleeve of his shirt and started to stand.

"Wouldn't do that if I were you. Just stay in your chair and answer my question. Now." Jamie pulled the trigger on his Colt 45 Peacemaker, hitting the ground inches from Billy's chair. Billy grabbed for his sidearm, but Jamie was too quick and a bullet hit Tankard's right wrist before he could touch the handle of his gun.

"Help me!" Tankard screamed to the others as he grabbed the now useless hand. "For God's sake, someone help me!" The men at the tables in the Silver Bell Saloon sat rooted in their seats. No one in the dusty desert hovel raised a hand to intervene. They'd all heard about MacLaren and his reputation as a fast gun.

"Now, dammit," Jamie demanded one last time as another shot just missed Billy's leg. "Believe me, Tankard, you'll feel the next bullet, and the next, until you tell me what I need to know." Jamie moved the barrel towards an area right below Billy's stomach.

"All right, all right," Billy relented, defeat in his voice. "But you're just gonna get killed over some whore that ain't worth..." That was as far as he got before a rock hard fist slammed into his face, breaking his nose. Blood gushed over Billy's lips and chin. He began rocking from side to side with his left hand covering his wounded face.

"What'd you do that for?" It was all Jamie could make out of Billy's mumbling.

"Tell me what you know, Billy. I won't repeat it again." Jamie cocked the gun one more time. The hostage may be many things, but Jamie doubted the woman he sought had become a whore since he'd last seen her.

The outlaw removed his hand to reveal eyes as wide as saucers. "I got held up in Blake Valley. Was s'pose to meet up here, but the gent," he gestured with his head toward the piano player, "said they left with the whor...I mean...lady, a few days ago. Didn't tell anyone where they were headed, but I'm think'n they rode south."

"Why south?"

"Cause that's where Hagan has his ranch. Holes up there when things get bad. It's in the hill area east of San Diego, but you can't get to him. The place is hard to find, guards everywhere. Only one way in and out. Nobody gets closer than a mile before the boys spot 'em." Billy paused, wincing at the pain radiating from his wrist.

"Go on, Tankard. I know there's more." MacLaren had a talent for flushing out information others couldn't, sensing things others didn't. Those talents and his lightning fast skills with a gun made him the best at finding those who had been taken and returning them to their families. He never gave up. At twenty-five-years-old, he was already the best.

Silence stretched between the two men. No one else in the saloon moved, all riveted on the scene before them. Billy swallowed hard, wiped his sleeve across his still bleeding nose, and coughed up blood.

"She's hurt. Bad. Got caught in gunfire over at Blake Valley. We all told Hagan to leave her, but he wouldn't," Billy scoffed, disgusted with the turn of events.

Jamie knew they'd taken the woman out of her San Francisco home four months ago. Hagan and his men had proceeded to ride throughout

California, Nevada, and Arizona to avoid detection while they continued their routine of robbing banks. He'd been hunting them the entire time.

"This was s'pose to be a quick kidnappn', get the money and cut her loose. Didn't work out that way. Hagan changed plans when the ransom wasn't paid. The boss didn't want to kill her. Refused to leave her 'cause he wanted her for himself. Doc said she'd never make the trip south, but Hagan wouldn't hear it. They went ahead. I was s'pose to meet 'em here. Used to be a good doc in this town, but he got himself killed a few months ago." Tankard stopped to glare at the lawman. "That's all I know. I swear it, MacLaren."

Sure it is. I've trailed your worthless hide long enough to know you haven't told me everything. The lawman had no doubt there was more, but he would get the rest out of Tankard on the trip south.

"Get up. You're coming with me." Jamie leveled his gun at Billy and motioned for him to stand.

"Hell no. I ain't going anywhere with you. Especially not near Hagan. He'll kill you, and me, and no one will lift a finger to help," Billy shook his head as he rose and started for the door.

"Grab your stuff, Tankard. You're leaving with me if I have to tie you to your horse and drag you to San Diego."

Billy scowled at MacLaren, but all the fight had gone out of him. He had accepted his fate. Except,

14

if he could mount his horse fast enough he just might be able to outrun the marshal.

"Don't even think about it, Billy. I'll catch you before you reach the town limits, then I will tie you to that horse." MacLaren scanned the street while he watched Tankard mount. He holstered his gun, jumped onto Rebel's back, and both men turned south toward San Diego.

Chapter Two

Hagan strolled over to the small bed. Victoria Wicklin felt the thin mattress sink from his weight as he sat down on the edge and looked at his hostage. She was wrapped in dirty blankets that covered her motionless body.

Victoria watched him through veiled eyes. Miguel never felt remorse, took what he wanted, killed when needed, and lied with more ease than any man she'd ever met, except, perhaps, her husband. *My husband*, she thought with bitterness. *Hopefully, someday, he will rot in hell.*

"You are better today, I think. Si, querida?" Miguel brushed strands of hair off her face as he spoke.

Victoria scooted further away, unable to stand the stench of the man who'd captured her. "No, Miguel. I'm still not well. My body aches all over and my head pounds most of the time. I need to rest and sleep," Victoria lied, hoping to discourage the disgusting man's advances.

Hagan's property was located deep in a maze of mountain passages, at the end of a protected canyon. A good-sized expanse of pasture existed between the entrance and the dilapidated house, assuring all visitors could be spotted with ease, as could those trying to escape. Still, Victoria was determined to find a way out.

At least Miguel no longer desired to bed her. He'd forced himself on her two months after the abduction when it seemed apparent her husband wouldn't pay the ransom. His men had stood guard outside the filthy upstairs room in the saloon. Even if she'd been able to stop Miguel, his men wouldn't have let her leave. Two more months had passed, and although he kept her with him, Miguel hadn't taken her again, perhaps still hoping that Wicklin would produce the money.

Then, three weeks ago, she'd been caught between Miguel, his men, and an angry rancher the outlaw had cheated in a card game. Hagan was unaware the rancher hadn't come alone. His sons, standing quietly at the bar, were also present, and what the bandit had thought would be a quick dispatch turned into a battle that left one of his men dead and several people wounded, Victoria included.

Victoria hadn't regained consciousness until they had arrived in another town. The pain overwhelmed her. Given what she'd learned of her captors over the past few months, it had surprised her along with everyone else that Hagan hadn't abandoned her to face death alone. But he'd kept her with them as they traveled south to the mountains of San Diego. No one knew how she'd survived the trip. Miguel ordered one of his men to bring a doctor, and after two weeks, although her energy was low, she felt healed, but she would never admit it to Miguel.

"You are a beautiful woman, Victoria. I should not have stopped after one time, I think. Tonight I will have you again." The sneer on his face turned her stomach.

Victoria remembered the other night and shuddered. At first she'd fought, before she'd realized her pathetic attempts were useless. He'd been angry with her, the way she laid on the bed without moving. He'd slapped her, called her foul names. Victoria had forced herself to focus her mind elsewhere, on another man, long ago, and ignore the pig on top of her.

"No, Miguel. It won't be any different. You'll find no pleasure from me." Her steady voice belied the panic she felt. Victoria looked away and stared at the wall next to her bed.

She knew he'd been visiting at least one of the girls he kept at the ranch to cook, clean, and entertain his men. Sofia's beautiful, long, dark hair, and her full figure captured Miguel's attention whenever he saw her. She had always been Miguel's woman when he lived at the ranch and Victoria's arrival hadn't changed the arrangement. Despite that, Sofia remained hostile. Victoria sympathized with her, but there was nothing anyone could do. She would leave if Miguel would allow it.

"Please, Miguel, let me return to my life in San Francisco." She swiveled her head away from the wall toward him when he rose from the bed and paced to the window. "Hamilton will never pay what he owes you. I'm of no value to you anymore and I'll never provide the pleasure you seek from your women." She knew the contempt in her voice wouldn't fall on deaf ears, but his next words were flung at her in cold fury.

"Make no mistake, querida. You are mine for as long as I want you," he bellowed. "I have decided I want you again. Do you understand or must I show you?" Miguel stalked towards her, removed his belt, and now stood a mere foot away.

"No, Miguel." Dread filled her voice. "No demonstration is needed."

Miguel replaced his belt, pulled on a coat, and started for the door. "I will return for you tonight. You will be ready for me, querida. This time you will welcome me to your bed."

Victoria's back stiffened. She remained on the bed, rigid, until long after Miguel had left. She couldn't stand another time in bed with that man. He'd threatened her before but never followed through. Many nights she hadn't slept, but lie awake, planning her escape.

Soon. It would have to be soon.

Chapter Three

"Stop fussing, Tankard. You're worse than traveling with a woman." Jamie's patience had been exhausted as he listened to the prisoner's constant complaints.

"Hell, Marshal. We've been travel'n with just short stops for days. I'm tired and sore. My horse needs to rest and I'm hungry. Like I told you, they ain't goin' nowhere. Hagan will stay there for a couple of months and rest up." Billy was a good rider. He'd spent long days and nights in the saddle, but traveling non-stop with a throbbing, broken nose and torn-up wrist was taking its toll on him. Besides, he had no intention of going all the way to Hagan's ranch with MacLaren. If the man had a death wish fine, but Tankard wanted no part of it.

"No rest until we get close to the ranch. How much longer?" Jamie was worn-out, but he'd learned to survive on short catnaps and little food while doing his work as a U.S. Marshal.

Jamie was an excellent lawman. He could locate missing people that others couldn't find, and no one was faster with a gun. Those he tracked always underestimated his skill, and many were dead because of it. He worked well alone, preferred it most of the time, as most jobs took him through several states and territories. No, the few days of little sleep or food on this trip wasn't what drained him. It was the hunt for this particular hostage.

Victoria. His ex-fiancée. The woman who'd married another while he was away. The woman he'd loved since he was sixteen and she fifteen. It had been seven years. The pain was still as intense as it had been when he first learned of her betrayal. Her actions had hurt many people and impacted many more. Jamie had left Fire Mountain a few short weeks after her marriage and ultimately became a U.S. Marshal. Now, due to his skill at recovering those abducted, it fell to him to find her. Return her to her family. Her husband.

Jamie had spent much of the past four months preparing to come face-to-face with the woman he'd never wanted to lay eyes on again. Now that his objective was only days away, however, he was filled with anticipation. He hoped Tankard could keep up the relentless pace.

"A day or two will put us a few miles from the valley entrance," Billy answered, even though he wasn't certain of the distance left to travel.

It won't be long now, Jamie thought.

******

Miguel hadn't made good on his threat. It'd been two nights, but he hadn't come for her. Victoria prayed this would continue, but knew it may not.

Tonight she felt much stronger. She'd overheard Miguel tell his men he planned to visit a neighboring ranch for a celebration to honor the rancher's recently betrothed daughter. Some of the men would go along, as well as Sofia, which was welcome news. A minimal number of men would be left to guard her and the ranch. According to Sofia's gloating words, these fiestas could last all night, so not to expect them until morning. But the taunts meant nothing to Victoria, other than to signal her chance had come. She'd hidden food and clothing. Now she'd wait until those left behind were occupied, and then she'd initiate her escape.

Yes, tonight would be her chance.

******

"We'll bed down here, Tankard. Get off your horse and sit by that scrub oak." MacLaren gestured to a bush a few feet away. "Hold out your hands." He retrieved his rope and knelt by his prisoner.

"You don't need that, Marshal. I ain't plan'n to take off," Billy protested, but did as the marshal ordered. Jamie secured Tankard's hands, then moved on to his feet.

"Dammit, MacLaren. I can hardly ride and my right hand is useless, and..." The rest of his words were muted by a kerchief stuffed in his mouth.

Jamie was through listening to the whining and constant chatter from this piece of trash. Finished, he stood, unsaddled Tankard's horse, but left Rebel ready to ride. They were too close to Hagan's ranch. He wouldn't take any chances by being careless.

Jamie walked to a rock out-cropping and worked his way through the rough-faced boulders. All he could see from this location was the start of a valley several hundred yards ahead with peaks on either side. He figured it must be the opening to Hagan's ranch. Now he understood why Tankard had thought it impenetrable. The canyon created a fortress, while the flat land for several hundred yards out provided little cover. A lookout would be able to see for miles.

Jamie had begun his descent off the rocks when he heard horses. It was near sunset, but he could still make out eight riders. They left the valley and turned north, away from his location, and continued around another hill until they were out of sight. From what he could see, there were six men and two women. He didn't know what that meant, except his chance may have come sooner than anticipated. Jamie hurried back to where Billy was trying to sleep and kicked his tied ankles, removing the gag with a quick tug.

"What d'you want?" Billy protested.

"How many men does Hagan keep with him?"

"I don't know. Eight, ten."

That meant there were no more than three, maybe four men still in the valley. Hagan could have added more. Didn't matter. These were still better odds than he'd expected.

Jamie checked his rifle and extra sidearm. Both were loaded and ready. He'd take Rebel, but also knew he'd be on foot much of the way to avoid detection. Jamie would go prepared. Now all he could do was wait.

******

All she could do was be patient and wait. Victoria went through her meager belongings once more. The group had left an hour ago but it still wasn't dark. She needed the cover of night for her escape to work.

She'd ventured outside the last two days, expressing her need for fresh air to Miguel. In truth, she wanted to gauge the distance to the valley entrance as well as the trails along the hillsides that surrounded the ranch. Although not tall, the scrub oak and occasional salt pine were dense. They'd provide good cover if she kept low. The problem would be noise. She needed a way to trek through all the underbrush without alerting the guards. Victoria turned to Miguel's trunk and located two pair of tattered, thick socks. She'd pack her shoes and wear his socks for walking, at least until she was beyond the valley opening.

Miguel had left two men behind. She knew from listening to Miguel's instructions that one man would remain posted at the entrance. He was short of men, having eight total. Two more women were still in the bunkhouse, but they were keeping the second man busy from the sounds Victoria could hear wafting across the open area between the buildings. She knew José had been told to keep watch outside the house, and was grateful he neglected his duties this night. He was a mean one, the worst of Miguel's crew. She didn't want to run up against him during her escape.

Miguel had been gone two hours. The sun was down, the moon a sliver in the darkened sky, and Victoria knew it was now or not at all. The back door off the kitchen was kept locked, but she'd found the extra key Miguel had stashed when he thought she was sleeping. Slipping outside, she closed the door and moved over the uneven ground until she reached a dense cluster of bushes far to the left of the house. She hid behind them and waited as several minutes ticked by. Nothing. No one had heard or seen her leave.

Victoria squinted as her eyes adjusted to the dark. There was a path along the backside of the scrub, perhaps an old deer path. The sight bolstered her courage.

She continued along the animal trail, taking cautious steps, avoiding fallen limbs, while moving among the rocks. At one point she heard the door of the bunkhouse open. José yelled something in Spanish to the women. She'd learned some of their language over the last few months but couldn't make out what he said. It didn't matter. José took a slow turn around the area, scanned for anything unusual, then, satisfied he'd done his job, walked back inside.

It took Victoria an hour to reach the opening that signaled her escape. She'd heard the men talk of it. A small cave nestled within the canyon walls. If followed it would meander through several yards of the mountain, then exit out on the other side toward a large rock formation. It dumped into the remains of a dried riverbed surrounded by dense scrub oak. The path paralleled the trail the men used when on horseback, but was hidden from view.

Victoria stopped to rest and looked up at the hill next to the valley entrance where the sentry was posted. No sign of Luis. It was dark. He might have moved further up the mountain, too far for her to see from this location.

This was her point of no return. She could head back now, with little chance of detection, or keep going into the more open plains where she'd almost certainly be spotted. Victoria continued on.

Chapter Four

Jamie made his way along the old creek bed, keeping near the trees that still held to life despite the arid conditions. Some were as high as twenty feet, but most were short and dense, providing excellent cover. He'd get as close as he felt safe, ground-tie Rebel, and continue on foot. Jamie estimated another hour to the valley entrance. After that he'd just have to take circumstances as they came.

Billy's description of the ranch area had been vague. The house, bunkhouse, old barn, and some fenced corrals were all laid out in a circle, with clear ground in the center. He knew the house would be the building farthest to the right as he entered, and that, he guessed, would be where the hostage was held. Hostage. It was best to think of her that way and not by her name. After all these years he still found the sound of her name painful, whether spoken out loud or a quiet thought.

Jamie continued forward a couple hundred more yards until he came to a spot where he felt Rebel would be safe and unseen. Grabbing his rifle and extra sidearm, he scanned the area once more before continuing on foot. About fifty feet ahead he saw where the creek bed made a sharp turn and the brush on each side came together. It was a perfect place to cross over so that he could enter the valley from the right. This was going better than expected. Perhaps his luck would hold.

******

Victoria continued on until the scrub oak became sparse. She considered her options. A couple hundred yards ahead stood a very dense stand of trees and brush. To reach it she'd need to cross a vast expanse of open space. It was a dark night, but Luis could still make her out if he were looking in her exact direction. She would take her chances. She replaced the two layers of socks with her shoes, steeled herself, grabbed her small bag and the hem of her skirt, and ran for the cover of the trees ahead.

The rocks hurt her feet, even through the shoes, but she continued to charge ahead as fast has her legs would travel. She didn't look back, but focused on her goal. She had to reach the trees. They were a hundred feet ahead when a bullet whizzed past. It hit the rocks to her right, sending up a small cloud of dust. She didn't slow her pace. They would have to kill her. She would not go back.

******

Jamie heard the gunfire and stopped. One shot, then nothing. He estimated it to be a few hundred feet ahead but realized it wasn't aimed at him. *Who are they shooting at?* He kept on, escalating his pace while scanning the area.

Another dense growth of trees and bushes lie just ahead. He focused on that area and continued forward, keeping low to the ground. Then he heard it. Someone or something was in front of him, making considerable noise as it moved through the scrub.

There was something else. Riders were headed in his direction, shouting, but he couldn't make out the words.

He arrived at the stand of trees just as the noise ahead of him stopped. Jamie could hear labored breathing, but that was all. He took cover behind a thick oak and leveled his rifle in the direction of the sound. The shouting continued in the distance, but his focus was on the possible danger in front of him.

******

The dense cloud cover made it impossible to see. Victoria stopped, took in huge gulps of air, and tried to make out the shapes a few feet away. Her heart raced as she tried to quell her panic. She needed time to think. The shouts drew closer. They knew she'd fled. The only weapon she had was a knife that had been left on a table, in plain sight. She'd stuffed it into her bag.

Her heart rate slowed somewhat and she began to formulate a plan. The brush was thick in this area. Perhaps she could find a place to hide, wait them out. Maybe one would turn back to find Miguel. That would leave her with just one man to fight. The only people she'd ever fought were her husband and Miguel, but she was scared and desperate, and determined to never go back. At this point she knew deep in her heart that she would kill, or die, to keep her freedom.

Victoria opened her bag, retrieved the knife, and started forward into the dense growth. In less than a minute she came to a small opening. She'd need to be quick to avoid detection. She stepped forward, knife in hand.

******

Jamie heard it again, this time much closer. Heavy gasps accompanied by breaking twigs. Whatever it was, it moved straight toward him, just beyond the small open space ahead. Heavy cloud cover obscured the moon. It was almost pitch black. He waited. No sense moving when he had good cover and his rifle aimed straight at the noise. He'd dispatch it, deal with the riders from the valley, and continue ahead to retrieve the hostage.

******

Victoria surged forward just as the clouds parted. Moonlight washed over her. She stood exposed in the clearing. A rifle cocked and she froze.

"Don't move." Jamie spoke just loud enough for the figure in front of him to hear. He could make out the form of a woman, but she faced away from him. It was still too dark to see her features.

Then the clouds broke free and she turned towards him.

Jamie's hands clenched tight on the rifle. He couldn't get a breath as he stared into the eyes of the only woman he'd ever loved, the woman he would have given anything and everything to have, the woman who'd betrayed him. She was stooped, as if in pain. He braced himself against the emotions that swept over him and stepped forward, never lowering his weapon.

Victoria gasped as she stared down the barrel of the rifle aimed at her heart. Her eyes moved up to the face of the man holding the gun. The eyes, the stance, the hair peeking below the hat tickled at her memory. There was something familiar about this man, but she had yet to place him. She lifted the hand holding the knife, but he mistook it as a challenge.

"I wouldn't, Torie," Jamie said in a deceptively casual voice as he continued to walk towards her. "You know how accurate I can be."

Victoria stood rooted in place. Only one person had ever called her Torie. The man lowered his rifle just a few inches and her breath caught. *My God, it can't be. Not here, not now.* The boy she'd loved in her youth, the man she still loved, was now a threatening presence standing in front of her. Her heart pounded in her chest. Jamie MacLaren.

After all these years he still took her breath away. Even with his rifle pointed at her, his expression inscrutable, he was still the most attractive man she'd ever seen. His dark whiskey-brown hair was a little long, and in the sunlight she knew there would be streaks of deep copper. He had a slight beard, as if he hadn't shaved in several days. She couldn't tell if his eyes were still a beautiful soft gray with deep steel colored rings, but she'd wager they were. Eyes that turned almost black when he was angry. His words began to penetrate her straying thoughts and she lowered the knife to her side.

"Drop it, Torie," he commanded.

"No, Jamie, I won't." The words were steady but strained.

The sound of her voice after seven years cut straight through him. "So you do recognize me. I wondered if you would." Jamie responded just as the shouts of men were heard nearby. He could hear them dismount and move in their direction.

"Get over here. Now." Giving orders and being obeyed were natural to him, but Victoria stood frozen in place. "Victoria, move over to me so I can protect you." His calm confidence pulled Victoria from her trance. She stepped next to him. Years of working to free hostages kicked in and he lowered his voice even more. "Good girl, now get behind me." This time she responded instantly.

Both slipped behind the shelter of the oak. Jamie used one hand to apply pressure to Victoria's shoulder as he indicated for her to crouch behind him, low to the ground. He placed a finger to his lips as a signal for her to stay silent.

His gut clenched as he watched her shudder, but she did as he instructed.

Two men crashed through the bushes, neither expecting to see a man with a rifle leveled at them.

"Stop right there, gentlemen. Not a foot more or I'll have you on the ground before you can spit." Jamie inched around the tree for a better angle.

"Ah, señor, we mean you no harm. We are chasing a woman. She belongs to our friend. He owns a ranch nearby. She is only his whore but we are afraid she has become lost." Victoria recognized José's voice and winced at his description of her. He was a liar and a cold-blooded killer. He wouldn't hesitate to add Jamie to the list of men who had died at his hand.

Whore? The outlaw's words slammed into Jamie but he shook them off. "By shooting at her? I doubt it. Why don't you just turn back and tell your boss you lost her? If I do find her, I'll send her back to you." He anticipated they wouldn't take the deal, but he needed time to edge his way to a spot where he'd have the best chance of dropping both men.

"That will not work for us, señor. He will kill us if we do not return with her." This time it was Luis. He was more reasonable but still a thief and murderer. "No need for violence between us. We are all men. We know how crazy women can be, si? She is loco. We know you have her, señor. Give her to us and we will let you live. Unless the woman means something to you?"

"The woman means nothing to me," Jamie replied without hesitation, "but that doesn't mean I will let you kill her."

José raised his gun as two shots echoed through the small clearing. Victoria screamed. She was stunned to find Jamie still standing. She looked ahead. José and Luis crumbled, almost as one. Both were dead before they hit the ground. It had all happened in less than two seconds.

"Torie, do you hear me?" Jamie hovered over her and reached out his hand to help her up. "Torie, we need to leave. Now. I have a horse but he's a ways back. Come on." Jamie's tone hadn't changed since his stinging words to José and Luis. *The woman means nothing to me.*

Victoria took his hand, grabbed her knife and bag, and started to follow him. He set a fast pace through the scrub and rock. A couple of minutes later she stumbled as she tried to keep up.

Jamie turned to see that Victoria wasn't behind him. He found her panting, but still attempting to will her shaky legs forward. He shifted the rifle to his left hand, circled her waist with his right and pulled her close against him. She winced in pain.

"Stay with me, Torie. We'll get out of this, but you need to stay with me this time." His words came out almost as a plea. *This time.* She raised her eyes to his and nodded. They'd make it. She would not go back. To either Miguel or her husband.

Chapter Five

It took only minutes to retrieve Rebel and ride back to where Tankard was working to free his bonds. "Not trying to escape are you, Billy?" Jamie dismounted and indicated with his rifle that he saw what the outlaw was doing.

Billy's mouth was still stuffed with the cloth that had been shoved into it, but he shook his head fiercely from side to side.

Jamie saddled Tankard's horse while Victoria waited atop Rebel. Once finished, he fished his long knife from the saddlebags and walked toward the bound man. Billy's eyes went wide before Jamie grabbed his ankles and cut the rope.

Jamie left Billy's hands tied and marched him over to his horse. "Mount up, Tankard." He waited until the man grabbed the horn with his tied hands, worked his left foot into the stirrup and swung over the saddle. As Jamie walked back to Rebel, Tankard kicked his horse and took off towards Hagan's ranch.

"Damn it, Billy," Jamie yelled. "Get back here."

He lifted Victoria down, mounted Rebel, and took off at full speed to either catch or kill the idiot who rode off with tied hands and no weapons.

He didn't ride long. Billy had come across the bodies of Luis and José, blood still oozing from their prone bodies. Jamie caught up with him within a few seconds and grabbed the reins from the man's shaking hands.

"You do this, Marshal?" Billy managed to get out.

"I did, Billy, and I won't hesitate to do the same to you if you pull a stunt like that again. Now, we're heading out and I don't want any more aggravation from you."

"Shit, MacLaren. You know Miguel won't let this go. He'll come after you and after the woman. We're all dead people." The fear in Billy's voice was tangible as Jamie rode ahead, leading his companion's horse behind him.

Jamie claimed the outlaws' guns and horses, and within an hour the three were miles from Hagan's ranch, heading to San Diego.

******

"Who's the woman, MacLaren?" Sheriff Huntsman nodded toward Victoria as they locked Billy in a cell. Jamie was mighty glad to get rid of him.

"Just someone who was kidnapped and held for ransom by Miguel Hagan. You know him?" Jamie hoped the sheriff had some interest in going after Hagan and his men.

"Sure do. A real hard case. Always seems to slip through our hands. You wouldn't happen to know where his ranch is, do you? His neighbors won't give him up for anything. He pays everyone well to keep silent. Kind of a local hero, you might say." The sheriff's tone reflected disgust. "We're shorthanded so I'll take any kind of help I can get."

"No problem. I know how to get you within a couple hundred yards of the entrance. You'll need more than a few men, though. His place is a fortress. Wish I could go with you. Nothing I'd like better than to wipe that piece of filth from the earth, but I need to deliver the woman to her kin and get back to more important business."

The sheriff looked at Victoria, but her focus seemed to be on the happenings outside. "Sure is a pretty thing, even if she is a bit beat up." Huntsman took a seat at his desk and motioned for Jamie to take another.

"Don't get taken in by her looks, Sheriff. She's no outlaw, but she's not an angel. Woman's left her share of deceit behind her. I'll be glad to get her to Fire Mountain and off my hands."

Whether intentional or not, Jamie's words carried through the office to where Victoria sat fiddling with a handkerchief that was dirty from use. She winced at his words. She knew Jamie hated her and would never understand why she'd made the one decision open to her seven years ago. If only she had the chance to change the past, but it was a futile thought. She'd live with her mistakes, and the pain they had caused, as best as she could.

"Probably best to take the railroad up to San Bernardino, then head east from there. Not another train heading north for two days, but it's worth the wait."

Two days. He didn't want to wait that long but he had no choice. "That'll work. Just need your signature on the prisoner release and we'll be on our way. Know of a hotel you'd recommend?" Jamie was ready for a hot meal and soft bed. A soft woman, too, if he could manage it. Being this close to Torie, without being able to touch her, ask her about the past, was more than he wanted to deal with twenty-four hours a day until they reached Fire Mountain.

"Florence Hotel is good. Clean and reasonable, with good food in the restaurant. Plus, my cousin Esther runs it. Give her my name and she'll take good care of you." He smiled then held out his hand to shake Jamie's.

"Thanks, Sheriff." Jamie headed over to where Victoria remained seated.

"Let's go." His voice was abrupt. The friendliness he'd shown the sheriff now gone.

******

Dinner was an excruciating affair. Jamie charmed the staff and thanked them for the great food. He never offered his guest a word or look. She sat in silence, eating little and wishing they could return to the room he'd secured for them. One room, but big enough for a bed for her and a daybed for him. She wouldn't even be able to shut a door so he could be out of her sight, and her thoughts, for at least one night.

"Ready?" Jamie wiped his mouth and tossed his napkin on the table. He stood and walked

38

around to pull out her chair. His sudden manners seemed absurd given that he hadn't acknowledged her all evening.

"Thank you," was all she could get out, and even that was said just above a whisper.

When they reached the room Jamie ushered her inside, grabbed his coat, and started for the door. She glanced at him with a question in her eyes.

"I'll be back later." He exited the room, closing the door soundly behind him.

She didn't understand why his sudden departure bothered her so much. Victoria had felt alone for most of the past four months, but this was a different type of feeling. It was more an emptiness at his absence. She'd wanted to reach out and ask him to stay. She didn't know why, perhaps just to be near him. But it would've been futile. She knew he'd have ignored her request and left anyway.

At least now there'd be quiet to calm her jagged nerves. The bath she took earlier had helped. The more time in his presence, the less confident she became that she could handle the long trip back to Arizona in such close proximity to the man.

He looked much the same. He'd always been more serious than his older brother, Niall, or his younger twin brothers. Now his disposition reflected a man who'd experienced more than he should have at his age. Jamie was harsh, wary, and closed. She'd tried to speak with him during their brief stops before arriving in San Diego, but he had cut her off with a look each time. He was professional and courteous, but unapproachable.

She walked to the bureau, changed into a gown and wrapper the hotel owner had offered, and lay down on the soft bed. She hadn't slept on anything so nice since being kidnapped. This wasn't first class, but it was far above the hard ground and lumpy pallets Miguel had provided over her four months of captivity. Victoria thought of Miguel and wondered if he would be angry or relieved that she was no longer his concern. The first was her guess, as Miguel saw women as nothing more than property. She had no doubt he believed he owned her. Perhaps, Victoria hoped, he'd decide she wasn't worth the effort to get her back. She wanted no more bloodshed on her account.

******

"What'll you have, honey?" The red haired woman in a bright green dress asked as Jamie settled at the bar. She was good looking and Jamie's mood picked up as she moved closer.

"A whiskey, darl'n'." Jamie looked at the shapely woman of about twenty standing before him. He'd come in for one drink, but hell, it'd been a sparse few months, and he was due.

"A whiskey for the gentleman," she called to the bartender.

"Sure enough, Betts."

"And one for the lady." Jamie looked at the bartender who nodded and plunked two shot glasses in front of them.

"To tonight, darl'n'." Jamie wrapped an arm around the saloon girl's waist and raised his glass. The pretty lady responded in kind.

"To tonight, handsome." Betts nodded and relaxed with the knowledge she'd found her partner for the evening.

******

"So tell me how you know that handsome lawman, Mrs. Wicklin. He sure has the female staff gawking." Esther, the hotel owner, poured some coffee the following morning and sat next to Victoria in the dining room. "I'm Esther Thomas and I own this hotel. Do you mind if I join you?" She asked as an afterthought.

"Not at all." The company of another woman, a respectable woman anyway, had happened just one other time in the four months she'd been Miguel's captive. Their conversation had lasted but a few minutes, long enough for Miguel to spot the two of them together and scare the other woman off. "I'd enjoy the company. It's been a long time since I've had a civil conversation with anyone."

"You mean Marshal MacLaren isn't civil to you? Seems real friendly to everyone around here." The woman's surprise showed on her face.

"Oh, he's civil. Does his job and leaves me alone most all the time. But it's been awhile since

I've spent time with another woman," Victoria explained without offering details.

"I heard from my cousin, the sheriff, that you'd been a hostage of that scoundrel, Miguel Hagan. The man should be hung for treating you the way he did. But now you're free and headed home. To Fire Mountain, in Arizona, is that right?" Esther took a sip of her coffee.

"Well, yes. At least long enough to visit my parents, but then I'll need to travel back to San Francisco. That's where I've been living for several years. From there, well, I just don't know..." Victoria's voice trailed off as her mind tried to deal with all that had happened.

"Mrs. Wicklin, I've been looking for you." Jamie's voice cut through the fog and she looked up to focus on his stern face but didn't reply.

"Good afternoon, Marshal," Esther said filling the lull in conversation.

"Afternoon, ma'am. I hope the woman hasn't been pestering you." To Jamie's embarrassment the hotel owner gave him a disgusted look.

"What would make you think that, Marshal? Mrs. Wicklin and I've been having a nice chat, at least until you arrived," the woman said. "Well, if you two will excuse me, I need to get back to business. Good day, Mrs. Wicklin. I do hope the rest of your journey home, wherever that takes you, is an improvement."

"Thank you, Mrs. Thomas. It's been my pleasure to share time with you." Victoria refused to give the marshal so much as a glance. "Well,

Jamie, you sure know how to make friends. You used to be quite the gentleman, but I see that's changed over the years."

"Oh, that's not all that's changed about me, Victoria. I'm sure you'll find that I'm not at all the same person I was at eighteen." Jamie didn't elaborate further before changing subjects. "I thought we'd have an early supper. We'll take the morning train tomorrow. Need to be on our way by seven."

Jamie followed the same routine that night after he deposited Victoria back in their room. Betts was accommodating, didn't ask questions, and spent the night tending to Jamie's needs. Just killing time, he'd convinced himself. There was no way he planned to spend an evening in a hotel room with a woman he didn't like or trust. They'd be on the train the next morning, headed for home, and it was coming none too soon for him.

Chapter Six

"Hen?" Tom entered the hotel lobby and found the owner at the front desk. "Hen, you aren't going to believe this. He found her. Marshal MacLaren found Victoria and they're on their way here," Tom gasped as he handed the telegram to Victoria's father.

"My God. Anna!" Hen turned to open the office door behind him. "You need to come out here. We have news." His hands shook from the unexpected telegram. It had been over four months since Jamie left to find their daughter. His regular updates kept them current, but there had been nothing in three weeks.

"Hen? What is going on that you need to yell?" Anna walked out from the back office shaking her head.

"It's word from Jamie, Anna. He found her. Good Lord, Anna. The boy found her."

"You're sure, Hen? There's no mistake?" The hopeful words from his wife tore at his heart. She grabbed the message to read the words for herself.

"Yes, sweetheart, I'm sure. Jamie wouldn't have sent word to us unless he had her with him." Hen's smile was wide but Anna couldn't control her tears. Four months since word of Victoria's kidnapping. Seven years since her marriage to Hamilton Wicklin, the last time they'd seen her.

Anna dried her cheeks with the handkerchief Hen offered, and smiled before taking a deep breath. "When? Do we have any idea when she'll be here?"

"Looks like tomorrow, Anna," Tom offered up as he stepped to the door. "Well, I best head back to the office. Knew you folks would want to see that right away. And great news it is."

"Thanks, Tom. And we'll expect you at the homecoming party we plan to throw once she's settled." Hen grabbed Anna and swung her around before depositing her in front of him for a reassuring hug. "Looks like we'll have our daughter back, sweetheart."

"Yes, Hen. Looks like we just might."

******

The trip had turned into a nightmare for Victoria. Jamie's treatment had continued to worsen. He had withdrawn more and more and now he didn't even acknowledge her. He seemed to go out of his way to shut her out, seldom responded to any question she asked, and refused to sit anywhere near her. She'd reached her limit.

"Jamie? Do you plan to ignore me the entire trip, treat me as if I'm some leper who will infect you if I venture too close?" Victoria had walked down the train aisle and sat in the empty seat next to him.

Jamie pulled his eyes from the window to look over at the subject of his latest daydreams. God, she was still as beautiful as he remembered. Honey

45

gold hair—the color of wheat—and striking violet colored eyes rimmed in a deep blue with gold specks. The years hadn't changed her. It was obvious that life with Wicklin wasn't the insufferable experience Jamie had hoped. No, Mrs. Victoria Wicklin appeared to be happy in her choice to marry for wealth and a life that included maids, butlers, and cooks. Oh, he knew what her life was like. Contrary to what Niall and others thought, he'd done what he could to learn her reasons for abandoning him to marry a stranger.

As it turned out, however, Wicklin hadn't been a stranger, but an old family friend. His aunt, Beatrice Wallace, and Torie's parents had been friends when they all lived in St. Louis. Both families were in the hotel business, each operating successful and opulent establishments that catered to wealthy businessmen and travelers. Each family was considered among the elite of St. Louis society.

Victoria's parents hadn't embraced that lifestyle. A few years after their marriage the two decided to leave for the burgeoning town of Los Angeles, but Anna became ill and the Wright's had made it no further than Fire Mountain. Hen used some of his considerable family money to open the best hotel in the area and a mercantile next door that catered to the many new families arriving from the east.

Not long after Hen and Anna decided to head west, Beatrice Wallace moved to San Francisco with her husband, opening hotels that had added to their mutual wealth. Her husband had died a few years after their arrival. Not long afterwards, Mrs. Wallace's sister died, leaving Beatrice with sole custody of her nephew, Hamilton Wicklin.

When Hamilton turned twenty-one, Mrs. Wallace had communicated with Hen and Anna over several months about a mutually beneficial marriage between Wicklin and Victoria. It had been Jamie's misfortune to learn nothing of these machinations until after he'd asked Victoria to marry. He'd never mentioned to Hen and Anna what he'd discovered.

"Jamie? Did you hear me?" Victoria queried after several minutes of continued silence.

"What is it you want to discuss, Victoria?"

"Well," Victoria said as she twisted an old handkerchief in her hands, "It just seems that we could at least be civil to each other. Maybe take meals together. I know it's not a long trip, but it might go faster if we share company." She didn't know what she'd hoped to accomplish, but the tension between them was unbearable.

"Civil to each other, huh? Perhaps I should explain my job to you, Mrs. Wicklin. I'm a U.S. Marshal. My job is to find kidnap victims, return them to their families, and move on to my next assignment. It's not to become friends with them, coddle them, or concern myself with their affairs in any way." Jamie's eyes moved over her body, stopping at the curve of her breasts, then continued their journey to her face. His soft grey eyes had turned to dark steel as they locked with hers. "Of course, if you are bored and offering to entertain me, then perhaps we can work something out." His smile was feral and had the desired effect. He saw the shock register as Victoria absorbed his meaning.

Her stomach tightened at his words, but she sat in silence, staring at him, resisting the urge to slap him. "No, Jamie, I'm sure I couldn't give you the type of entertainment that Betts provided in San Diego," she said through clenched teeth. Jamie had the good graces to appear embarrassed at the news that Victoria wasn't unaware of how he'd spent his nights in the California town. "I obviously misjudged you and the extent of your hatred for me. You are an insufferable lout. Please, go back to your brooding existence and forget we even spoke." Victoria rose to leave when Jamie's hand flew out to grab her arm.

"Sit down, Victoria." Jamie chuckled as she lowered herself back into her seat. "Insufferable lout, huh? I see you haven't lost any of your fiery temper in all these years."

Victoria let out a disgusted sound as she sat next to him, twisting the piece of cloth in her hand.

"And what is that you keep messing with?" Jamie started to reach out to take it from her, but she was too quick and pulled away before he could grab it

"Nothing. Just an old memento I keep with me. You'd never understand."

"Perhaps not. I certainly never understood you, or what was important to you. But it appears the choice you made years ago suits you fine and you've no regrets." The words were measured, devoid of emotion or accusation. "I just don't see that we have anything to say or reminisce about. Your folks will be glad to get you home, at least for a while, until you leave to be with your husband in San Francisco." He sat back into the seat and lowered his hat over his eyes. He hoped it would shut out the woman next to him. It worked.

Victoria said nothing. She sat anchored to her seat, his words washing over her. Painful words that pierced her heart and brought back all the bad memories of why she'd left—why she'd had to leave—all those years ago.

******

News about Victoria traveled fast. Most of the town knew to expect her back on today's stage. Hen found it impossible to focus on his work. The hotel door opened and he looked up to see Niall and Kate MacLaren walk in carrying two-month old Adam. Seven-year old Beth ran in behind them, followed by Kate's father, retired marshal Trent Garner, and Niall's twin brothers, Drew and Will.

"Hey, Mr. Wright." Beth's excited voice carried throughout the hotel lobby.

"Well, good afternoon to you, Beth. And how are you doing this fine day?" Hen smiled warmly at the pretty, exuberant little girl.

"We're all great, aren't we, Papa?" Beth gazed up at her father.

"Yes, Beth, we're all great." Niall held his hand out to shake the one Hen offered. "Spoke to Tom. He said the stage should be here within the hour." Niall's smile was broad. This could be the best news anyone had received in a long time. And now, maybe there would be a way for Jamie and Victoria to talk things out and put to rest the pain Jamie had tried to hide the past few years.

"Here it comes!" They all turned at the announcement from outside. Fire Mountain had grown to over a thousand residents and it seemed that nearly all of them had turned out to welcome Victoria home.

"Well, mother, I guess it's time." Hen reassured Anna with a smile, took her hand, and walked toward the stage office.

******

"Five more minutes," Jamie said.

Victoria didn't answer. She just nodded her head and continued to stare out the window. The landscape was so familiar. A few more ranches, more houses. The town looked like it had expanded beyond the borders of seven years ago. It was still beautiful and familiar.

Jamie had worked hard the whole trip to ignore Torie. It had been a miserable journey with both of them doing their best to act as if the other didn't exist. She was still the most distracting woman he'd ever met. Her dark, golden blond tresses were piled on her head, but he remembered what they looked like when they flowed over her shoulders. Her eyes were still the same pale violet that darkened when she was angry or filled with passion. The last thought had him straighten in his seat, readjusting himself. Although they'd never consummated their love, there'd been many times when they had brought each other intense pleasure. He forced himself to remember that those were just old memories. She wasn't the innocent girl from their past. And she wasn't his, hadn't been in many years.

Victoria wondered what her parents would say to her as the stage drew closer. Would they accept her, knowing what had happened over the past four months? The past seven years? She loved them so, but would they ever understand why she'd had to do the only thing acceptable seven years ago? Would they forgive her? Could she forgive herself? Her fear of what to expect was almost crippling, but she would not let Jamie see how distressed she was, or how his continued silence sliced at her heart.

"Whoa." The driver's voice rang above the pounding horse hooves.

She clutched her bag, took a deep breath, and ventured a hesitant look at Jamie. Would she see him again once they arrived, or would he complete his assignment and ride out of her life? If she were honest, it was what she deserved after the way she'd treated him all those years ago. Oh, how she wished things had been different.

"Victoria, did you hear me?" Jamie looked at her with eyes devoid of emotion, his voice flat. "We're here. Time to get out and greet your folks."

That's when she heard the cheering. She shrunk back into the coach, looking at Jamie for an answer.

"Just your neighbors. They've come out to welcome you home. Might as well face it now as they're not going anywhere." No smile, no warmth. He held out his hand again to help her down. This time she complied.

As her feet hit the ground and she looked up, Victoria stared into the eyes of the man who had raised her, taught her right from wrong, and did all the things that good fathers do. "Papa." Victoria said with only the hint of a smile.

Her sad, terrified eyes pierced Hen's heart. He'd always been a perceptive man, and his instincts told him that his daughter, the light of his life, didn't know if she'd be accepted.

"Victoria, welcome home." Hen opened his arms wide. It took her only a moment to rush into them. The tears started as she clutched her father's arms and settled into his embrace. She looked around him and her eyes landed on her mother. She turned and was wrapped in another welcoming hug.

"Oh, Victoria, sweetheart. We've been so afraid for you, and missed you so much. But now you're home where you belong." Her mother's soft words washed over Victoria. For the first time in many years she felt a sense of peace.

Jamie stood aside to watch the reunion. It had been a long time coming. He started to turn away when he heard a familiar voice. "So you found her. Nice job, son. We're all glad you're home." Trent Garner slapped his former protégé on the back.

Trent had known Jamie and his brothers, Niall, Drew, and Will, for over thirteen years. He'd met the boys after their parents were murdered and their Ohio farm destroyed. The boys had been too young to witness such carnage. The four were traveling across country to reach their uncle's ranch in Arizona when Trent spotted them getting off a train in St. Louis. He'd taken a liking to them and had stayed in touch all these years. He'd retired not long before his daughter, Kate, married the oldest MacLaren brother, Niall, last year.

Jamie turned to grasp the hand of the man who was instrumental in his decision to become a marshal. Trent Garner had taught the boys how to handle a gun, and encouraged them to stand on their own. It had been welcome news when Jamie learned Trent had purchased a ranch not far from the MacLaren spread, and hoped maybe someday he would find a reason to return, and be near his family and Trent.

"Hey, Trent. Four months of following the worthless trash, but finally caught up to them in the San Diego desert. Only regret is that I didn't get the leader, Miguel Hagan. I found Mrs. Wicklin, though, so I'm satisfied with the outcome." Jamie still felt conflicted about not getting Hagan. He'd decided the risk was too great once he'd found Victoria. She was home now and his commitment fulfilled. He'd leave soon and she'd be back to what she was supposed to be, just another memory.

"Uncle Jamie!" He was brought back to reality by two small arms wrapping themselves around his waist. The lawman looked down to see his seven year old niece, Beth, clinging to him with a bright smile and two missing teeth.

"Beth. How is my favorite niece?" Jamie bent to pick her up and swing her around.

"Uncle Jamie, I'm you're only niece." Beth hugged her uncle and laughed.

"Welcome back, Jamie. Glad you're safe." His older brother, Niall, stood beside their twin brothers, Drew and Will. They'd all come to town for the homecoming.

"Thanks, Niall. Glad to be home." And Jamie meant it. For several years he and his older brother had been at odds on just about everything including cattle, chores, the twins, anything that could have two opinions. Each brother ended up on the opposite side of the other. Jamie knew much of it was his fault and hoped to set things right with his family.

Niall lowered his voice. "So, how is she, Jamie? Did you find out any more from her during the trip home?"

Jamie glanced over at Victoria and her parents. He was happy for Hen and Anna, glad they could see their daughter after all these years. "I believe she'll do okay, but nothing was said about the past. She didn't offer any explanation for her actions, and honestly, I didn't ask and don't care. She's on her own now and I expect she'll be heading back to her husband in San Francisco before too long."

"I doubt that, Jamie." Sam Browning, one of Jamie's friends and a deputy in Fire Mountain walked up. "Welcome back. Nice work."

"Thanks, Sam. What do you mean you doubt she'll be heading back to San Francisco?" Sam's comment had gotten everyone's attention, and fast.

"Well, the lady may be going back to San Francisco, but not to her husband. We got word Hamilton Wicklin's body was found in the bay with several bullet holes. So, guess she won't be heading back to him." Sam knew some of the history between Jamie and Victoria, but not a great deal. Their split had happened before he'd come to town. But one thing he did know; his friend was still in love with the woman.

"Murdered?" Niall asked.

"Appears so. Don't have details. Wicklin was declared dead and, according to the telegram, the lady is now a widow. Sheriff Rawlins plans to go to the hotel later to inform Mrs. Wicklin. Don't envy him that job. Well, I'd best be getting back to the office. Come by and see me when you have time, Jamie. We'll head to the Desert Dove for a drink." Sam turned towards the jail.

"Hey, Niall, why don't Drew and I take Beth to the mercantile and grab the supplies Aunt Alicia needs?" Will asked as he took his niece's hand. The twins were good at sensing when the two older brothers needed time alone.

Niall just nodded as the three walked off. "I'll be damned. Murdered." He digested the news and possible implications. "What do you think, Jamie?"

"Hell, I don't know what to think, other than I know for certain it changes nothing between Victoria and me. She didn't want me seven years ago and has no feelings for me now. It's over. I'm sorry she's a widow, but the woman is out of my system," Jamie lied. "Care to join me at the Dove for a drink? I need something after the past few days." He sounded tired and somewhat defeated, two traits seldom associated with the lawman.

"Can't now. Got the family with me. But you better be out for dinner. Aunt Alicia's making your favorites and you don't want to disappoint her." Niall smiled and placed a hand on his younger brother's shoulder. "Glad you're back. Real glad."

Chapter Seven

Several days had passed since Victoria's arrival and the news of her husband's death. She'd be a hypocrite if she pretended to mourn Hamilton's passing. No, she wasn't sorry he was dead. Victoria was curious more than anything. Why was he killed, and in such a gruesome fashion? She knew he had enemies, lots of enemies. Ham wasn't a popular man. He'd been treated with tolerance if not acceptance in San Francisco because of his aunt's legacy. But murdered?

Her husband's attorney had identified Wicklin by items that had been found on his body. There wasn't much, only an engraved pocket watch, keys to his office, and tokens. Victoria was sure the tokens were for Madeleine's, a brothel he patronized on a regular basis. Regardless, the San Francisco police continued to look for the killer.

"Victoria, I'm going out to the MacLaren's right after dinner. I'd love for you to come along. You won't believe how Niall has improved the place over the past few years. I know they'd love to see you." Anna had asked her daughter to accompany her someplace each day, but had been politely refused every time.

"Thank you, Mama, but I'd rather stay at home. I'm still tired and don't feel like facing anyone." It was a lie. She wanted to see Jamie again, but only if he came to her. There'd been no word from him since their arrival and the news of her husband's murder.

Anna sat down next to Victoria and laid a hand on her daughter's arm.

"You're a grown woman and must deal with life as best you can, but your father and I are worried about your decision to stay in your room day after day. You avoid everyone. Are you ill? Is there anything we can do to help you?"

What could she say? There was so much she wanted to tell her parents, but so little she felt she could share without humiliating herself and them. She hadn't wanted to leave all those years ago, but circumstances had dictated it. So much had happened during her seven years in San Francisco. Her kidnapping and abuse by Miguel Hagan had only added to her desolation. She didn't know how to explain the treatment she'd received by her husband and the outlaw to her parents without incurring their pity. And she did not need pity, just acceptance. There'd been so much pain and disillusionment, she truly believed she'd never be the person her parents remembered.

"No, Mama, I'm not ill. I just need more time. I know the MacLarens will understand if I don't come with you." At least she hoped they would. Was Jamie still around, or had he already left the area?

"Well, I don't know about that. I believe at least one MacLaren would like to see you."

"And who would that be, Mama?" Perhaps her mother had received news.

"Jamie, of course. I understand he's taken a leave from the U.S. Marshals Service to help his brothers build another barn and add a room to the house. I'm certain he'd want to know you're settling in okay."

"He told you that? Asked about me?" Victoria couldn't believe the man who'd had brought her home felt anything for her at all.

"Well, no. I haven't seen him since you arrived. But that's not unusual. None of the MacLarens come into town much except for business or supplies, but that doesn't mean he's not thinking of you."

"Believe me, he isn't thinking of me, or wasting one moment wondering how I am. He came after me from a sense of duty———it's his job. I spent several days traveling with him, and there's no doubt that Jamie hates me, Mama. Who could blame him? I married someone else and threw away all the plans we'd made. He'll never forgive me, and I'll never forgive myself." She'd said too much. No one needed to know how much she still loved him.

Anna considered what else she could say to help her daughter cope with all that had happened. "You may be right. None of us really know how that boy feels. But I'll tell you this, he left town within weeks of your marriage and took up with some rancher in New Mexico as a hired gun. Made good money. We heard he took his trade to Texas and did real well. That boy was always fast; faster than the rest. He was earning himself quite a reputation as I understand it. Thank God he ran into Marshal Garner, because that boy was headed for bad things. Garner straightened him out, got him involved in the Marshals Service. They use him for situations others can't handle, such as finding captives just like you. He's turned into one fine young man."

"I know, Mama, and I understand that none of that would've happened if I'd kept my promises to him. I failed him, but he's made a good life for himself. Much better than mine." Her tone was resigned, as if her life was over and nothing good could come of it after all that had happened.

"Honey, you know you can talk to me. I won't judge you. It's hard to help if I don't understand how your life has been since you left." Her mother's expectant tone almost had Victoria opening up to share the decision she'd made to conceal her failings. But she just couldn't do it. She knew her secrets were hers alone and not to be shared with anyone, especially the three people who meant the most to her.

"Please don't worry. I simply need more rest and time to adjust to the fact that I'm a widow. I'll need to travel to California at some point, but for now, I'd prefer to enjoy the peace of being home and the comfort of your company. Can you understand?" Victoria loved her parents. She didn't want to cause them any further pain.

"Of course, darling. Do what's needed to get your life in order and move on. Your father and I will support any decision you make." Anna kissed her daughter's cheek. Victoria had yet to offer anything about her past. She spent most days in her room, just coming down for dinner and supper, and not taking breakfast at all. The only other constant was the way she fidgeted with a handkerchief that never left her possession. Anna had only gotten a glimpse of it. The initials JM were embroidered in one corner.

Chapter Eight

Jamie hammered one board after the next into the wall frame for the second barn. The ranch had grown under Niall's management and the family had made the decision to breed and train horses for the ranchers in California. As he hammered, the events of the past few months played through his head.

How he wished someone else had been assigned to find Victoria. It had taken time, but he'd learned to live with the knowledge she'd never loved him. Torie's dreams were grander than being married to a rancher in a small Arizona town. The answer to her dreams had materialized in the form of Hamilton Wicklin just days after Jamie had proposed and ridden out of town. One look at life outside of Fire Mountain, away from him, and she'd jumped at it.

As he continued to work, his mind drifted to something else and his stomach twisted. The brief words Billy Tankard had thrown at him in the desert saloon. He'd called Victoria a whore. Jamie hadn't believed it, thought they were just the words of a scared man. Then the outlaw he'd shot in the desert outside Hagan's ranch had called her the man's whore. *What had Miguel done to her?* Jamie had spent so much time trying to distract himself, he realized he'd never asked about her treatment during captivity. It was a basic question, one he asked all freed captives. *Why didn't I ask her?*

"Need some help?" Drew approached with more nails and a jug of water.

"Help and water are always appreciated." Jamie smiled at his younger brother. He was glad for the distraction from his deteriorating thoughts.

"You've made a lot of progress since dinner. You're working like a man possessed. Want to share your thoughts?" Drew was the most compassionate of the brothers. He was a hard worker, good wrangler, smart, and possessed an abundance of empathy when he sensed someone was troubled. He planned to leave for college soon, and Jamie knew how much the family would miss him.

"Just reminiscing, that's all." Jamie took a deep swallow from the jug Drew offered.

"Tough thing to have to rescue a woman who messed up your life. Don't know that I could've done it." Drew shielded his eyes from the sun as it descended behind the mountains.

Jamie was surprised his younger brother had any notion of what had transpired. "Didn't think you'd remember too much of it. You were only what? Ten when Victoria left town?"

"I may have been young but I wasn't stupid. You were different with Victoria. More settled, less volatile and, well, less of a pain. But everything changed when she left town. It was obvious, even to Will and me, that something terrible had happened. Then you took off. It was hard on all of us, Jamie." Drew had started to pound nails into another board as he spoke, but Jamie heard the slight censure in his brother's voice and winced for the hurt he'd caused his family. Victoria's deceit had impacted a lot of people.

Jamie walked over to Drew and laid his hand on his shoulder. "I was selfish, Drew, and didn't know how to handle myself. Made some bad decisions, but things turned out all right, didn't they?"

"Don't know yet, Jamie. Can you handle her being back in town? Will her being here cause you to visit even less? If so, that would crush Aunt Alicia." Drew's voice was even, without the bitter undertones Jamie expected.

"Victoria means nothing to me any longer. She's just a kidnap victim, a woman I found and brought back home. You already know her husband was found dead, murdered. She'll either stay here or head back to her life in San Francisco. Who knows? It makes no difference to me. Any feelings I had for her are long buried."

"Well, if that's your story, big brother, I'll accept it. I hope to God you're right." The brothers worked another hour in silence, both realizing the future was far from certain.

******

"Great supper, Aunt Alicia." Jamie stood to help clear the table. "Besides the family, your cooking is what I miss most about being gone."

"Well, you could always turn in your badge and come home." Alicia smiled over her shoulder as she washed dishes.

"I've thought about it. It's been five years and I don't know if I'm up for another five. Guess I'm not the man Garner is."

Trent Garner had still been a U. S. Marshal when he'd pulled Jamie out of a bad situation in Abilene. Jamie'd almost been the victim of a crowd hanging before Trent intervened and talked reason to the angry mob.

Jamie had been cleared of any charges, but not before Garner had given him a choice. He could handle the charges himself or the marshal would speak for him, but only if Jamie agreed to join the Marshals Service. The decision had been an easy one and the best thing he'd ever done. Now Trent had a ranch near theirs. Not long ago a series of events had brought Trent's daughter, Kate, to the MacLaren ranch. Niall and Kate, after some missteps of their own, had married and produced another male, baby Adam, for Alicia to nurture. "Oh, don't fool yourself. You're as good a man, but you also have a whole family that wants you here and would be elated if you stayed. We won't pressure you, but want you to know what you mean to us." Alicia's eyes teared but her smile was pure warmth.

Will walked in just as the last dish was being placed in the cupboard. "You gonna stay in here all night, Jamie, or join the men for a brandy?"

"You offer whiskey and I'm there." It was good to be home, Jamie thought, but could he handle it now that Victoria was back?

Chapter Nine

"Why, Jamie, it's good to see you." Hen had just closed the cash box when Jamie walked into the hotel lobby. "You have business in town or just come by to visit?"

"A little of both, Mr. Wright." He returned Hen's smile. The man seemed younger, more alert than Jamie had seen him in a long while. Victoria's return must be working out well for her parents. "I had some business with Sheriff Rawlins. Thought I'd stop to see how Victoria's doing. If she's settling in okay."

"You mean, how is she handling her husband's death?"

Jamie's look of chagrin made Hen's smile widen.

"Don't know I'd have said it that way, but yes. Is she doing okay after getting the news?" He'd been able to keep his curiosity under control over the past few days, but the truth was, he couldn't stop thinking about her. "Rawlins said no one has seen much of her since the stage arrived."

"She's struggling a little, trying to reconcile the change in her situation, I guess. Victoria doesn't talk much about it. She hasn't spoken a dozen words since her arrival about her husband or her treatment by that outlaw." Hen's worry was etched in his face. He shook off his concern and walked around the guest counter. "Gerald? I'm leaving. You all set to take over?"

"Sure thing, Mr. Wright. I'll take care of everything." Gerald said from the back room.

"Jamie, why don't you and I head over to the house? We can visit on the way and perhaps Anna will have some pie waiting when we get there."

"I appreciate the offer, Mr. Wright, but I'm not looking to intrude. Don't want Victoria to think I'm prying into her business." Although his desire to see Victoria was strong, he sure as hell didn't want to be the first to make a move. The way Jamie had it figured, if she had any interest in setting things right, explaining the past, she needed to come to him, not the other way around.

"You're not prying and certainly not intruding. Stop by for a few minutes, have some coffee at least, and give an old man a break from all the woman talk."

How could Jamie refuse the request from another man to save him from another night of female banter? He couldn't. "Fine, Mr. Wright. As long as you don't think it'll cause problems, I'd like to stop by for a spell."

The walk wasn't long and not much was said. Jamie didn't want to push and Hen didn't want to pry.

"Anna, we have company. Do you happen to have any more of that pie left?" Hen called out as the two men walked into the spacious kitchen. Hen had practically grown up in the kitchens of large hotels. Two generations of Wrights before him had managed some of the grandest hotels in Boston and then St. Louis. As a boy, he'd spent hours in the kitchens, learning how they operated and making friends with the hotel staff. The lessons learned had served him well. Although their kitchen was not as large, it was well equipped, and was the model of efficiency compared to most kitchens Jamie had seen.

"Jamie, how are you?" Anna asked as she walked over to greet her husband with a quick kiss on the cheek.

"Good, Mrs. Wright," Jamie replied but his eyes had fixed on the other figure in the kitchen who stood not six feet away, straight backed, with a smile that appeared hesitant or forced, Jamie couldn't decide which. "Hello, Victoria."

"Marshal MacLaren," Victoria replied. Her voice was strained, whether from sorrow or something else. Jamie didn't know.

"Now, Victoria. I believe you may call the marshal by his first name, right Jamie?" Anna looked at one and then other of the two young people, waiting for a reaction.

"Yes, that'd be just fine, Mrs. Wright." His eyes never wavered from Victoria.

Hen took a seat at the large, sturdy, kitchen table. "Okay then, pie all around. And coffee if you have some, Anna. Come on, Jamie, sit wherever you'd like. Victoria, you too, sweetheart. Did you get to visit anyone today?" Hen could tell Victoria was struggling between a decision to stay in such close proximity to Jamie or to make some excuse and leave. He hoped her good graces would win out.

Victoria knew her parents expected behavior that had been taught to her since she was a young girl. The lessons had served her well as Hamilton's wife in San Francisco, a role she'd despised. She started to decline when a stern look from her mother changed her mind. "No, Papa. I didn't have an opportunity to visit anyone. Perhaps tomorrow." The tension seemed to drain from the room as she settled into a chair next to her father.

"Jamie, tell us what's been going on at the ranch. Heard the MacLarens have about exhausted the wood supply at the lumberyard." Hen eyed the large piece of pie Anna placed before him.

"Don't doubt it. Niall has us building a second barn, additional training areas, and an upstairs bedroom for Adam with room for a housekeeper. Niall's worried Alicia is working too hard. Of course it's beyond her to ask for help, so the best approach is to simply build a room and hire a housekeeper. She'll have a fit but, in the end, I believe it's the best for her. Niall thinks Will's going to ask Emily Jacobson to get married, and they'll live at the ranch, at least until Will can build a house of his own. And you all know Drew's heading off to college in a few weeks. Lots of changes."

"Emily and Will, huh? Well, I'm not surprised. Those two have been close for a long time now," Anna interjected as Jamie shoveled pie into his mouth.

Victoria watched Jamie enjoy her mother's cooking and remembered many other nights, just like this one, when they'd all sat at this same table. Even as a boy he'd been a voracious eater. It seemed so long ago. The news of Will and Emily had been a surprise, but the stab to her heart when she heard of their plans was a jolt. Not because of Will and Emily. The announcement reminded her of how it had been with Jamie, the two of them years ago with the same plans and dreams his younger brother had now. She hoped their plans worked out better than the ones she and Jamie had made.

"Thank you, Mrs. Wright. That was excellent." Jamie stood to put his plate on the counter.

"So glad you liked it. Here, I'll take that." She extended her hand. "Why don't you and Victoria go out on the porch? Get some air while Hen and I finish up in here."

"Oh, that isn't necessary. I'm sure he has other plans, right, Jamie?" Victoria wasn't ready to be alone with him and hoped he'd take the opportunity to leave. At the same time, a part of her wanted him to stay.

Jamie thought he heard something in Victoria's voice. Was it hope that he'd leave or hope that he'd ask her to join him outside? "Well," Jamie replied as he worked to decipher the tone of Victoria's words, "sitting outside for a bit sounds real good to me. If you have the time."

She nodded as he walked to the door and held it open for her.

The two sat in silence for long minutes, each trying to find the words needed to breach the gulf that had formed so long ago. He thought of the pain, the lost years, his anger at Torie's actions. She thought of the man now sitting beside her, so much like the boy she remembered, but so different.

"Would you like to walk for a while? I need to stretch my legs." Jamie rose and held out his hand to help her up.

"Of course." Victoria's gaze focused on his outstretched hand. It was just an offer to help her up, but for some reason, she wanted it to mean more. A moment passed before she took it to stand then released it just as quickly. His touch, after all these years, still produced intense sensations that shot straight through her. She wished it didn't. "Do you ever go to the river? The knoll?"

The knoll. He hadn't thought about the small hill overlooking the river in a long time. That's where he and Victoria had always met to get away, to be together. Not a far walk, but it had seemed miles away when they were teenagers. It was the place they had been together for the last time, before he'd left town with his brothers. It was where he'd asked her to marry him.

"No, I haven't been there in years." Even though his mind fought it, his legs began to move, almost by memory, to their spot on the knoll.

Several more minutes passed before she spoke. "Do you get here often? Back to Fire Mountain, I mean?"

"No, only about once a year, if that. My job keeps me moving around." He was glad to focus on something else, anything but the woman who walked not a foot away from him, and memories better left forgotten.

"You seem to have a particular talent for the types of assignments you're given. Do most of them involve finding victims such as me?" They'd reached the top of the knoll. The memories were so thick she didn't think she'd be able to remain, but knew turning back would accomplish nothing.

"Most do involve finding people who've been taken from their families. The only constant is that all the families have money. They're all wealthy, like you. Money is a powerful lure. Most people can't seem to ignore it." Jamie didn't realize how his words sounded until he'd spoken them. He cringed. Perhaps Victoria hadn't noticed.

She didn't respond right away, but focused on the river a few feet away. She needed time to compose her words, think through how to say what should've been said so many years ago.

"I know you must hate me. What I did, to you, to us, was unthinkable. There's no excuse except, at the time, I thought it was the best decision, the only decision." She walked a few paces then turned to face Jamie. "I didn't leave because I no longer loved you. I loved you more than you'll ever believe. But there were circumstances that forced me to marry Wicklin and..." She stopped as Jamie closed the small distance between them and grasped her shoulders. He wasn't rough, but she could feel the power radiating through him.

"Oh, I understand. You may have thought you loved me, but you loved Wicklin's money more. It was clear to me at the time, and it's clear now. You made the only decision you could under the circumstances. We both knew that I'd never be able to provide the kind of life that Wicklin offered. You saw your chance and you took it. Don't try to wrap it up any other way just because you're now his widow." He dropped his hands but continued to stare at her. His eyes narrowed and he shook his head in disgust at what he saw as an obvious lie. The bitterness in Jamie's words cut deep into Victoria and she realized she might never be able to reach him.

"You just don't understand what happened. He gave me no choice."

"Is that so? Then tell me what happened. What was it that forced you to abandon our dreams and marry him?"

His voice was calm, too calm after the heated words thrown at her just moments ago. That should've warned her. Victoria walked away from him to the edge of the riverbank. She could feel rather than see Jamie come up behind her. He placed his hands on her shoulders and in his own gentle way, turned her to him.

"Tell me, Victoria. Why did you leave if it wasn't for the money?" His voice was a whisper across her face. She could almost smell the anger pulsing from him, along with all the other familiar scents of the man she'd always loved. He was just as intoxicating now, just as impossible to resist.

She lifted her face to his to look into eyes that had turned a deep steel grey. She could lose herself in those eyes. It was her last coherent thought as his mouth moved towards hers inch-by-inch, brushing across her lips, and coaxing them to open for him. When she didn't resist Jamie moved one arm to the back of her neck, holding her in place while his other arm moved to her back, pressing her to him. Her arms slid up and around his neck, pulling his head down to hers. His mouth moved to her eyes, traveled across her checks and down her neck, before settling again on her parted lips.

Jamie was amazed at how the taste and feel of Victoria in his arms hadn't changed. She was still the most desirable woman he'd ever known. No matter what else had transpired, his body still craved hers as it had none other.

His hands moved down her back, over her hips, caressing them, encouraging her to relax. As he sensed her melting to him, his fingers moved down her leg and started to draw the folds of her dress upward until the only barrier between his hand and her thigh was a thin chemise. A deep moan from Victoria stopped his progress, brought him back to the present. Jamie dropped his hand, let the material fall back to her ankles. He once again grasped her shoulders with a light touch to push her away before stepping back with a ragged breath.

She stood rooted in place, her glazed eyes open and fixed on his. Neither spoke. Reality came back to her in small increments. The initial kiss, his lips across her face as his strong arms encircled her to draw them together. His slight beard scraping her cheeks, sending pulses through her body. One hand sliding down her back, pulling on the fabric of her dress. All the sensations she'd fantasized about for all those years. But he'd stopped.

"We'd better get back." It was the only explanation he gave.

She blinked, trying to restrain the tears that were just on the surface, waiting to spill onto her cheeks. She wouldn't let him see the effect he had on her. Nodding her understanding, she began walking at a brisk pace down the hill towards her parents' home.

"Torie, wait," Jamie called, but she didn't pause, didn't look back. Just kept moving with dogged determination to reach the house and the safety it offered.

The door slammed shut behind her. Jamie could hear the lock as it was moved into place. Even though he'd wanted to talk with her about her time as Hagan's prisoner, he didn't try to stop her. Her refusal to turn back to him when he called had made it plain he'd done the right thing by stopping what had been about to happen. She would have let him take her. He knew it. And it would have been wrong for them both. This couldn't happen again. He needed her to tell him the truth about the past. Perhaps then he could put it all behind him and decide whether or not to ride out of her life for the last time.

Chapter Ten

"Hey, Sam. What brings you out this late?" Niall was surprised when the deputy arrived just after supper.

"Niall," Sam nodded, shaking the offered hand. "Need to speak with Jamie if he's around." His voice was somber.

"Sam, what's going on? Would you like a whiskey?" Jamie had walked up behind Niall with a full shot glass in his hand and extended it to his friend.

"That'd be great. Thanks." Sam accepted the whiskey and Jamie motioned him into the study where the others were seated.

Sam looked around, gauging just how much he could say in front of Drew and Will. He kept forgetting that they were now men, and mighty fine men at that.

"It's about Mrs. Wicklin. There're some complications about her husband's disappearance and her kidnapping." He looked at each of them but would leave it up to Jamie if he wanted the others to stay.

"Go ahead, Sam." Jamie trusted his family. He had no misgivings about discussing any news with them in the room.

"Well, it appears that Wicklin's alive." The room went still at Sam's words. No one made a sound as all eyes focused on the deputy. "Not only that, he's claiming his wife's kidnapping was a hoax, and that she was behind the attempt on his life so she could collect his aunt's inheritance. I received a letter from Wicklin's attorney, but with Sheriff Rawlins out of town, I thought it best to come out here, get your take on it." Sam took a step forward, grabbed the whiskey bottle off the desk, and poured one more round for everyone.

Jamie sat dazed, pondering what he'd just heard. No matter what kind of person she had become, it was hard for him to imagine Victoria involved in a murder plot. He was still grappling with her passionate response to him last night on the knoll, deciding what to think, how to react. Now this.

"I thought he was reported dead. They found his body. Identified him. How do we know this isn't some type of hoax?" Drew asked, surprise registering on his face as he tried to process the accusations. "And, if it's true, where's Wicklin been all this time?"

"Don't know where he's been, but that's one of the things I mean to find out. It's pretty complex. Wicklin says someone tried to rob him while he walked home along the docks. The robber took Wicklin's possessions and was ready to leave when a third man stepped up, shot the robber, and pushed the corpse into San Francisco Bay. According to Wicklin's attorney, the robber was about the same height and build as his client, and with the stolen items on him, everything pointed to the body being Hamilton Wicklin." Sam shook his head as if trying to organize the information for his friends. "Turns out the man who murdered the robber is none other than Miguel Hagan, Victoria's alleged kidnapper."

"Hold on a minute, Sam," Jamie interjected as he shot out of his chair. "Alleged kidnapper? I was there when she escaped from his ranch. She was running from him. She was the victim."

"But did you see her with Hagan? How do you know she was kidnapped? Or, did she go with him as part of a bigger plan to go after her husband? Maybe she changed her mind and decided to get away from Hagan once she realized she no longer needed him. Do you have any proof she was his prisoner?"

"You know I don't. Victoria had already escaped. Hagan's men were following, shooting at her, when she ran right across my path. They demanded I turn her over. When I refused, both drew on me," Jamie finished, but his mind was reeling with the questions Sam asked.

"And you killed them?"

"Hell, Sam, you know better than to ask that. I'm standing here, aren't I?" Jamie's temper rose, not at Sam's words, but at the implications of the charges. Everything he'd believed about the kidnapping might be a lie, and Victoria was at the center, again.

"Once the men were dead, did you go back to the ranch to check things out? Find any evidence that would prove Mrs. Wicklin was kidnapped and didn't accompany Hagan willingly?" Sam asked. He knew this was difficult for Jamie, and his friend was on a short fuse, but he needed answers if they were going to sort out this mess.

Jamie sat down on a nearby chair, his body slumped forward with his arms resting on his knees. He ran a hand through his thick hair then drew a deep breath. "No, Sam. I didn't go back to the ranch. All the information I had pointed to her being a victim. There was no reason to try to find evidence to confirm if it were true. I took her and Tankard to San Diego, deposited him in jail, and brought Victoria here. Assignment over." At least it had been for Jamie.

Niall hadn't said a word since Sam had relayed the news. He wondered how anyone could believe that Victoria would be mixed up in a murder plot. Yes, she left unexpectedly years ago, but should that be a factor in the charges being leveled at her today? "Attempted murder. That's quite a charge. Did the letter detail any proof?" Niall's words were void of emotion but his eyes were sparking with disbelief.

"The attorney says he has witnesses and the proof needed to put her in jail. There's a judge looking over the evidence. He's trying to get an arrest warrant out on her. No telling how long that'll take. Doesn't look good." Sam laid his glass down, grabbed his head and looked to Jamie. "Thought you should know, as I may have to arrest her."

"Before that happens, don't you think we ought to go talk to her, hear what she has to say? Everyone here knows my feelings towards her. I don't trust her and know nothing about what she's done the past seven years. She may be involved, maybe not, but she needs to tell her side of things." Jamie wouldn't allow what had happened last night to push him toward another mistake involving Victoria. She'd duped him once and he had no intention of letting her do it again.

"That's reasonable," Sam replied. "Give me a few days to see if I can find out anything more on Wicklin or Victoria. I'll be in touch." Sam nodded to everyone and strolled out the door, pondering the fastest way to get information before they confronted Mrs. Wicklin.

******

"Well, Jamie MacLaren and Sam Browning. Please come in. Would either of you care for coffee?" Anna had been ready to leave for the mercantile when the two men arrived.

"Thank you, ma'am. No coffee for either of us. We need a word with Mrs. Wicklin. That is, if she's at home." At the worried expression on Mrs. Wright's face, Sam continued. "We need to give her some information and ask some questions. Shouldn't take too long."

"Of course, Sam," but her eyes searched Jamie's for any clue as to what was happening. "She's in her room. I'll go get her for you." Anna turned to walk up the stairs but found her daughter standing by the railing, listening to the conversation below.

"Victoria, Deputy Browning and Jamie are here. Said they have more information and need to ask you some questions."

"I heard, Mama. Perhaps it's about Ham's death. Maybe they've found the killer." Victoria knew she'd felt nothing for her dead husband, not in the beginning and certainly not now. His death meant little to her other than she was a free woman.

Victoria followed her mother down the stairs and found the two men standing, waiting for her. Her first look at Jamie since last night was a jolt. She wondered if he'd felt the same intensity she had in their kisses. She doubted it, as he seemed to have been able to back away without a second thought. He was closed and aloof. Even though their trip to Fire Mountain had allowed her some time to study him, he had kept his distance, staying away from her as much as possible. Perhaps that is what had made their encounter last night such a surprise. She'd been ill prepared for the impact, or the let-down.

"Deputy Browning, Marshal MacLaren, you wish to speak with me?" It was Jamie who drew her attention. She focused on him, and again, his eyes were devoid of emotion. Both men nodded, but it was Sam who spoke.

"Yes, ma'am, if you have a few minutes."

"Of course, please sit down." Victoria gestured to some chairs. Sam took one, but Jamie continued to stand. "Coffee?"

"Uh, no ma'am. Just some of your time." Again it was Sam who spoke. "I understand when you left Fire Mountain seven years ago you'd just married Mr. Wicklin, is that right?"

"Yes. I married Hamilton and left for his home in San Francisco." She glanced at Jamie, but he made no indication that her words troubled him.

"And you were still married to him at the time of your kidnapping?"

"Yes, deputy, that's correct." Victoria wondered where this conversation was going. She'd thought they were here to tell her that they'd learned who murdered her husband, but now she wasn't so sure.

"I understand you were the caretaker of some property and funds his aunt, Mrs. Beatrice Wallace, left to you?"

"Well, yes. Ham's aunt left money available to us each year for living expenses, so we could remain in her house and continue to run the restaurant she and her late husband had started. Aunt Beatrice designated me as the one responsible for how the funds were spent. My authority has been limited. Almost every expenditure must be reviewed by her long-time attorney and her banker, even the restaurant expenses. Hamilton managed the day to day operations of the restaurant, but had no access to the funds provided by Aunt Beatrice." Victoria

84

could feel her defenses rise at the direction these questions were headed.

"Beyond that, as I understand it, you were the sole beneficiary of the remainder of her estate if you stayed married to Wicklin for at least seven years. Is my information correct?" The deputy's eyes focused on her, weighing every reaction. Jamie hadn't moved from where he stood against the far wall, but his eyes never wavered from her face.

"No. No, that's not correct. I only know of the annual allowance. There wasn't anything else and she certainly wouldn't have ever left it to me. Ham was her nephew. She raised him after his mother's death. That's who any other inheritance would've gone to." Panic began to tinge her voice and she started to fiddle with the handkerchief she always carried. Jamie's eyes moved to the scrap of fabric then shot up to her face. For the first time he noticed the initials JM were clearly visible on one corner. It was his handkerchief, the one he'd given her when they'd promised to marry.

"Are you saying you knew nothing about Mrs. Wallace leaving you her fortune? You didn't know you'd inherit all of it if you stayed married to Mr. Wicklin for at least seven years?" Sam's voice changed as his questions continued. They were still spoken in a soft tone, but with an edge, as if he didn't believe her.

"Yes, that's exactly what I'm saying. She left me nothing, other than to insist I handle the finances from the annual payments designated in her will. Don't you think if she'd left anything further that I would've been made aware of it?" Her temper rose and she fought to rein it in. Her temper and sharp tongue had always been her weakest characteristics. She could hold both in check a long time, but once released, they were almost impossible to stop before she said or did something foolish.

"Yes, you would think that, Mrs. Wicklin."

"Are you going to tell me what this is about, or are you just going to pepper me with questions concerning things I know nothing about?" When he hesitated, Victoria stood up from her seat and charged on. "I want answers, Deputy, and I want them now."

"That's precisely what we want, also, Mrs. Wicklin, and we aim to get truthful ones."

Victoria just stared at him. Her stomach clenched and her heart pounded in her chest. She worked to control her breathing before either man could notice how the questions were affecting her.

"Then perhaps you should leave and find someone you trust to answer your questions, because your tone has made it clear you don't believe me. Aunt Beatrice designated me to handle the annual finances. That's it. Period. But you probably already know that since I'm positive that two impartial lawmen such as yourselves would have contacted her attorney, Silas Dunsford." The lawmen glanced at each other as she stopped to take a breath. "Now if the two of you would please leave, I have things to do. Things that don't include being accused of lying."

"He's been found. Alive." Sam stated matter-of-factly.

"Who? Ham? He's alive? I don't understand. I was told he was dead, that they found his body. How could he now be alive?"

"He was found by a Chinese fisherman several weeks ago. I don't have all the details, but he wasn't in great shape. Don't yet know why it took so long for them to notify the authorities, but they finally did and he was able to prove he's Hamilton Wicklin."

She pondered this only a few seconds. "Chinese fisherman? I'm sorry, I don't understand." She stopped to think through the unexpected news, but there was only one good response. "Well, it's good that he's alive."

"You'll be wanting to see him, I suppose?" Sam continued in a low, cautious voice, not wanting to rile her any further.

"No. I don't want to see him, Deputy. Not ever again. I'm glad he's alive, but I've no intention of returning to him." Her voice faded as she realized she might, in fact, have to see Ham again, if only to settle the finances and complete a divorce. "I'll divorce him, but I'll never go back to him."

"Well, a divorce may be the least of your worries right now, Mrs. Wicklin."

Her head popped up from where she had been absent-mindedly twisting the fabric she held in her hands. "Why's that, Deputy?" Victoria asked but her stomach clenched again at the deputy's tone.

Sam stood and walked toward her, until he was standing only a few feet away. He needed to gauge her reaction to his next words. "He says you planned to have him killed, and fabricated your own kidnapping to avoid suspicion."

"What? That's ridiculous!" Victoria glared at him, her eyes not wavering as they met his. "I was kidnapped by Miguel Hagan because my husband reneged on paying Hagan money he owed him. I refused to pay the debt out of the annual funds. Ham was furious, threatened to do all kinds of things to me, but his threats no longer had the same effect as in the past."

She paused, thinking back on her life with Ham and her treatment at the hands of Miguel Hagan. She shook off the memories, took a breath and continued. "He was a cheat, a liar, a miserable human being, Deputy, but I would never have tried to kill him." She walked over to the settee, lowering herself with as much dignity as possible, but her mind was on the accusations. She realized her nightmare might not be over.

Her mother, who'd been in the next room listening to the entire conversation, entered, walked over to her daughter, and turned to face the two men.

"I want you both to leave. Now. I don't want either of you to ever step foot in this house again until you've come back to your senses." She looked down at Victoria, then continued. "She may have hurt you terribly, Jamie, but I never thought I'd see you stoop to such low tactics to get your revenge."

At that, Jamie's eyes snapped up to Mrs. Wright's, but he held his tongue as she continued. "She's been through an awful experience and you come here accusing her of things she could never do. And accepting the word of a scoundrel, someone his own aunt didn't trust, over Victoria's. How could you do this to her?" Anna glared at Jamie, the pain evident on her face, but he continued to keep his neutral.

At that moment the front door opened and Hen stepped in. The words he heard coming from Anna stopped him cold.

"Now leave. Don't ever come back. Either one of you." Anna's voice had lowered, but was just as hard. Jamie knew her well, and God help them if Wicklin's accusations turned out to be lies. He'd lose friends he'd known most of his life, very good people who deserved none of this. And Victoria would've suffered through a humiliating experience for nothing.

Sam motioned to Jamie and they headed for the door.

"Sam, Jamie, what's this about?" Hen asked, but the two just tipped their hats and walked past him.

"Anna? Victoria? Will someone please tell me what's going on?" His words fell on deaf ears. His wife sat, arms wrapped around her daughter, rocking her to help ease the pain-filled sobs that wracked Victoria's small frame. Anna looked up at her husband and shook her head, then rested her chin on Victoria's lowered head and kept rocking.

Chapter Eleven

Sam and Jamie walked back to the sheriff's office in silence, each lost in his own thoughts, trying to sort through Victoria's answers and what he'd observed. After several minutes, Sam broke the silence.

"I don't know, Jamie. I've talked to a lot of people who declared their innocence, and Victoria comes off as someone who knew nothing about the provisions in the aunt's will or the additional inheritance. From what I was able to find out, Wicklin doesn't have a great reputation, and I have to say, Mrs. Wright may be onto something. Why would his aunt leave the managing of finances to a woman she'd known only a few years at the time of her death instead of her nephew, who she'd raised? Unless, of course, she knew things about her nephew and didn't trust him. His accusations just don't make sense."

Jamie kept silent. Doubt and guilt plagued his thoughts. He'd been the one to push Sam to confront Victoria, but his history with her was so painful that he'd found it hard to be objective. He knew her for what she was—a woman capable of deceit.

"Don't forget she has a history of doing whatever she has to in order to get what she wants, Sam. Lying hasn't been beyond her in the past, and, in my experience, liars don't change. They just get better at it." Jamie had to get his emotions under control and look at the facts, at the history of the accused. According to Wicklin's attorney, she had significant motivation in the form of huge financial gain, and she disliked her husband. She made no excuses for it when they spoke with her. Besides that, a judge in San Francisco was looking at additional evidence and checking out witnesses. None of this boded well for her or her innocence.

Sam stopped and scrutinized at his long-time friend. He knew little of what had transpired all those years ago, but he knew that it still caused his friend great pain.

"Jamie, you may need to step back from this one. It may be best to let Sheriff Rawlins and me handle Mrs. Wicklin. No one but she and her husband know what transpired to get her to go with him all those years ago and I, for one, can't judge her on that. Right now we have to be objective and work off what we know and what we can still find out." He looked at his friend to see if anything he said was getting through. "Wicklin may be right, that she partnered with Hagan to arrange her own kidnapping. And he may be right that she talked Hagan into getting rid of him. She'd get the inheritance and the outlaw would get his money. But my gut's telling me otherwise. I need to know if you're able to help us, and be objective, or if you've judged and convicted her. I could sure use your help, but not if you've already made up your mind."

Jamie shoved his hands into his pockets and stared at the floorboards of the long walkway leading to the sheriff's office. Sam was right to bring this up. Was she innocent of the charges, possibly innocent of other things as well? Hell, he just didn't know any more. Looking up he saw that they'd stopped in front of the Desert Dove, a saloon his brother, Niall, had frequented before he married Kate.

"I need a drink, Sam, maybe several. Appreciate your words, but right now I need to wrestle with my own thoughts. Don't come looking for me; I'll get back to you." With that, Jamie headed into the saloon and the long bar.

"Jamie." The bartender greeted him. Ross had been with Gloria Chalmette, the saloon owner, only a few weeks, but he recognized the marshal right off. "What can I get you?"

"A whiskey, Ross, and leave the bottle." Jamie downed the first shot, then continued to pour himself two more before stopping for air. Hell, getting himself drunk wouldn't help him think, but it sure would dull the pain he felt at seeing Victoria's reaction to Sam's questions. Jamie knew she'd looked to him for help but all he'd offered was an accusatory silence. He could still hear Anna's voice telling them to never return. What a mess.

"Marshal, what brings you in here so early in the day?" Gloria walked up and gave Jamie a quick pat on the arm before motioning for Ross to bring her a glass. She'd owned the Desert Dove for several years and was just a couple years older than Jamie. "Mind if I have one?"

"No. Help yourself." Jamie didn't want company, but Gloria was almost like family, in a strange sort of way, and he didn't want to antagonize anybody else today.

They stood at the bar in an uncomfortable silence before Gloria spoke again.

"Word has it that your hostage is being accused of some pretty outlandish things. That true?"

"Ex-hostage, and how the hell do you know about that?" He couldn't believe word of this had already spread to the Dove, as locals referred to it.

"Now, Jamie," she chuckled, "you know how the saloon business works, especially in a small town. Alcohol loosens otherwise closed tongues. So, what's going on with the Wright's?"

"It's only Mrs. Wicklin, Gloria, and no offense, but it's none of your business." He downed another shot, turned, and rested his elbows on the bar, looking out at the almost deserted saloon. Two o'clock, too early for much business. That would change in about three hours when the locals and the few ranchers who were in town came by before heading home.

"Maybe not." Then she rephrased it. "Probably not, but you best know what you're accusing her of, and why, before doing anything stupid like arresting her for something most believe she'd never do."

Jamie just looked at her, and then the bottle. Hell, he'd get no peace here. Picking up the bottle, he walked through the doors and plunked himself into one of the chairs Gloria always left outside, poured another drink, downed it, then one more, and set the bottle on the walkway. He lowered his hat over his eyes, stretched out his long legs, and fell asleep.

******

What? Someone was kicking at him and pushing on his shoulders. His eyes opened to slits and he found himself staring at smiling, bright blue eyes, and blond curls. A small hand was patting his cheek.

"Uncle Jamie, you have to wake up. Aunt Alicia sent me and Papa to get you." Beth. It was his niece and his older brother, Niall. What now?

"Get up, Jamie. We've been sent to fetch you home. Supper's waiting and Alicia is on her high horse." Niall's words finally penetrated. Jamie began to unfurl his long frame from the stiff wooden chair and stand. It was pitch black outside. *How long have I been out, anyway?*

He wasn't an idiot, contrary to what his ex-hostage might think. Angering three women in one day was more than enough. Angering a fourth, who happened to be his aunt, well, he might as well just go out and shoot himself.

"Fine, I'm coming. Just let me get Rebel and we'll be off." Jamie's voice was scratchy from the alcohol and sleep.

"We already got her, Uncle Jamie. See?" Beth pointed to his paint standing in front of the saloon.

"Him, Beth. Rebel is a guy, not a gal." Jamie chuckled for the first time since this recent situation with Victoria had started.

He left the half-empty, forgotten bottle of whiskey on the wood planks and mounted Rebel. It was a short twenty-minute ride, but the way he felt it would seem like hours. He sat straighter in the saddle and prepared for the verbal lashing he expected at the ranch.

None of the three had noticed Sam standing by the side of the saloon as they mounted and rode out. He sauntered over to the bottle, picked it up, then headed straight into the saloon toward Gloria.

"Good to see you, Deputy. And how was your day?" Gloria's suggestive smile was not lost on Sam.

God, she was a gorgeous woman. Long, jet black hair, dark eyes, and creamy skin, all tributes to her Creole heritage. She was older than him by a year or so, but that didn't faze Sam. Neither did the fact that she owned a saloon and had, for a few years before that, been part of the group of ladies who entertained the men.

It had all changed when she bought the saloon from the previous owner. The whole town knew that since then she'd only been with one man, Niall MacLaren. Sam suspected that Niall had hurt her, even if unintentionally. He was determined to crumble her defenses, and if she'd let him, step in where Niall had left a void. Sam wanted her, and he suspected she knew it, but Gloria seemed to still mourn the loss of her long-time friend and lover.

"Could've been better." He paused a moment. "Much better." He glanced around the saloon.

Gloria watched Sam's expression. She knew whatever conversation had taken place with Mrs. Wicklin must have bothered him. His normally impassive face showed concern, confusion. She'd gotten to know him over the past several months and admired the way he handled his job. There were many other things she admired about him but she'd been cautious. It was obvious he liked her, wanted her.

Even though Niall's marriage was expected, Gloria's heart had still been bruised. She knew it was due more to the fact that they could no longer be friends. Now he barely acknowledged her. She'd cared for him, but she'd always known their friendship would never develop into anything permanent.

It was different with Sam. It had surprised her when she realized her feelings for him were stronger than what she'd felt for Niall. She wanted him with an intensity that she'd never felt for anyone. It scared her, but she'd decided it might be time to risk her heart, see what would happen.

"You going to finish that bottle, deputy? Because if not, I could be persuaded to have a pour." Gloria glanced at the bottle in his hand, then back up at this face.

"Sharing the bottle suits me fine. Ross, two glasses please."

Sam poured whiskey into the glasses, then handed one to Gloria.

"To you, Gloria, and continued success with the Dove," Sam toasted, and downed the amber liquid. Gloria drank hers then poured each another. Sam eyed her suspiciously. Gloria rarely drank while the saloon was open.

She lifted her glass. "To us." She looked into his eyes while waiting for him to catch on. When he did, his lips curved into a smile and he lifted his glass to hers. "To us." They each threw back the whiskey at the same time.

Sam watched her place her glass back on the bar, felt her hand slip into his, and saw her motion to the stairs. It was all the encouragement he needed. He followed her, for the first time, to the second floor. Neither of them noticed that all heads turned in their direction, followed them up the stairs, and noted, with apparent approval, a change at the Dove.

Chapter Twelve

He'd known supper would be unpleasant. Jamie sat at the supper table fielding questions he couldn't answer.

"But you've known her since you were twelve-years-old, Jamie, and you know there is no chance Victoria would go along with killing anyone. You do know that, right?" Alicia would not back off. He loved his aunt, but he couldn't answer questions about Victoria. For all he knew, there could already be a warrant out for her arrest.

"To be honest, I don't know what she is capable of, Aunt Alicia. It's been seven years. She's led a life none of us know anything about with a man who could be honorable or the devil incarnate," Jamie answered through clenched teeth as he continued to chew the steak that had lost all its taste.

"What's incarnate, Papa?" Beth asked as she fidgeted in her seat. Niall exchanged a glance with his wife, Kate, Beth's stepmother. She and Niall had been married less than a year, but Kate and Beth had become very close. Their son, Adam, was less than a year old, and quite a handful, as now, when he fidgeted on his mother's lap.

Kate stepped in at just the right moment as she looked over at her stepdaughter. "I could really use some help, Beth. Time for you and me to take Adam upstairs."

Now it was just Alicia, Niall, Jamie, and Drew at the table. The fourth brother, Will, had decided to visit his long-time girl, Emily. Most thought they'd be engaged within the next few weeks. Jamie wondered if he'd ever find someone like Kate or feel the contentment his brother had with his wife and children.

"Do you know anything at all about her husband, Jamie?" Niall wanted to get back to the accusations. Although he'd always liked Victoria, he'd been as angry with her as anyone when she'd walked out on his brother. But, unlike most others, he'd pushed for Jamie to go after her, confront her, and find out the truth of her decision. The brothers had fought over this on several occasions before Jamie had chosen to leave the ranch, and his family, behind.

"Only that he's a businessman in San Francisco. Manages the restaurant and bar his aunt started. Sam found out he's a big time gambler and loses on a regular basis. The interesting part is that he has quite a few friends in positions of power. People he may be able to go to when he's in a bind. Connections that would prove critical to a man like Wicklin." He looked at Niall and saw the significance register with his brother. "That's all we know at this point." It wasn't much, but it was a start.

"And Victoria manages the money?" Niall asked again.

"Sounds like she manages the annual allowance. The actual extent of the aunt's property is in question. Wicklin alleges there is more than just the house and restaurant. Apparently the entire estate is quite substantial. Unfortunately, the attorney the aunt used for years, and who handles the estate, is back east, visiting his daughter. Not due back for a few weeks. Sam sent a telegram to him at his daughter's place in Boston. We're waiting for a response."

Drew spoke up. "And the kidnapping? How does all that play into it?" Of all the MacLaren's, he was the most intellectual. He hated it when things didn't seem to make sense, and reveled in solving mysteries that puzzled others.

"Not sure." Jamie proceeded to tell them Victoria's version of the kidnapping. He had to admit that not once had it seemed like she was part of a setup. Even Tankard had talked about her in terms of being a hostage, not a willing accomplice. She'd appeared to be the victim right up until the time Hamilton Wicklin had made his accusations. If Jamie had been able to stick around long enough to confront Miguel Hagan, maybe he'd have the answers everyone needed. But he and Victoria may not have made it out alive. No, grabbing her when he did was for the best.

"Wicklin vanished a couple of months after the kidnapping. Claims Victoria fabricated her own abduction and worked with Hagan to setup Wicklin's murder." Jamie shook his head at the extent of someone's lies, but whose?

"Anyone corroborate his story?" Drew asked as he spooned apple pie into his mouth.

"There's a doctor to verify that some Chinese fishermen brought him to their camp once to treat an injured man. The doc didn't know the man's name, just that he was almost dead. It took Wicklin several weeks to recuperate enough to talk about his identity. He claims others saw Hagan attack him at the docks and heard Hagan say that Victoria wished Wicklin dead. The statements of these witnesses may be enough for some judge in San Francisco to consider issuing a warrant."

"And if she did do all he says, Wicklin stands to inherit everything instead of Victoria, right?" Drew asked.

"That's my guess." Jamie threw his napkin on the table and pushed himself out of his chair. God, he was tired. He just didn't know what to think.

Jamie reflected back on what he knew. He'd found her running from two men, but what did that really prove? Billy Tankard had told him straight out that Hagan had kidnapped her, and demanded a ransom in the amount Wicklin owed for an unpaid debt, the same story Victoria had told Sam and him when they went to the Wright's. Billy was in a San Diego jail, and unless they had already released him, Jamie still might be able to get his story on the record. Unfortunately, he doubted Billy would talk.

For Jamie, the most insurmountable obstacle continued to be the fact that she'd lied to him all those years ago when she'd said she loved him enough to marry him. Could she be lying about her true relationship with Hagan?

"I'll be heading back to town early tomorrow to review it all again with Sam. Don't know when I'll be back at the ranch. I'm sorry, Niall. I know you were counting on me to help finish with the building. I'll get back as soon as I can." Niall hadn't asked much of him since he'd left the ranch, except to come home when he could and help with constructing the new barn. He hated letting his brother down.

"Not a problem." Niall walked up beside him and rested his hand on Jamie's shoulder. "Finding out the truth about Wicklin's charges is more important right now. Come back when you can."

******

He loved watching her. Each time they were together it was better than the time before. They talked as if they'd known each other forever, sharing their dreams for the future and memories of their pasts. He found he couldn't wait to be with her each night. Sam was in big trouble. He knew he'd never walk away if Gloria gave any indication she wanted him to be a permanent part of her life.

"So, what's your timing, Gloria? You going to be looking to sell soon?"

They'd become friends during his time in Fire Mountain. Although she was the most beautiful woman he'd ever known it was her compassion, unwavering spirit, and fierce determination to help those who'd been wronged that seized his heart. He'd marry her if she gave him half a chance.

"I have enough saved up to sell anytime. Then I'll leave, find a new home, and a new identity far away from here." It pained her to think of leaving the life she'd built, but it would need to be done if she had any hope of meeting someone who'd love her. How she wished it could be Sam. She loved him, but knew he'd found a home here and good friends in the MacLarens. Even if he did love her, he'd never give up his job for a former saloon owner and whore.

He listened quietly as she talked about leaving. It hurt Sam to hear her plan a future that didn't include him. Maybe it would make a difference if she loved him. He was sure she still had feelings for Niall and even though she never brought up his name, Sam could feel his ghost in the room, in this bed, most nights.

"You could stay, build a life here after you've sold the Dove. People like and accept you. It's not like a lot of towns I've been through. You've done well for yourself, Gloria, and everyone knows how much you've given back to the town. Don't throw it away so easily."

"And do what, Sam? Live in a small house on the outskirts of town and grow a garden?" She laughed but her eyes didn't reflect amusement. He was right about the town, however. Most folks here were more tolerant of her profession than elsewhere. But still, it'd be expecting too much to think they'd be able to forget her past and accept her as one of their own.

"Get married, have children. You do want that, don't you?" Sam hoped her answer would somehow give him the encouragement he needed to tell her how he felt.

"Yes," she admitted in a quiet voice. "But who would I marry? I want love, Sam, not some meaningless marriage so I can be considered a respectable woman. Maybe I'll be able to find it somewhere else." How she wished Sam would say something to indicate he had feelings for her beyond the passion they shared in bed.

"You don't believe you could find it here? Love?"

"With who? Jerrod Minton, Josh Jacklin?" She named men that Sam knew. Jerrod was the town's most successful attorney and Josh was Trent Garner's foreman. Men everyone respected, but men she didn't and could never love.

"Hell, no." His answer came fast and firm. "With me."

She couldn't contain her surprise. "You, Sam?" Gloria stared at him wide-eyed as if what he asked was unthinkable.

"Yes, me. Is the prospect of having me as your husband so awful?" If he didn't convince her to stay she'd sell the Dove and move away, looking for love in another town with another man.

A wide grin formed on her face and then faded to one of resignation as the reality of their situation returned. "No, the prospect of you as a husband is not awful at all. But your job is here and I don't know that the town will ever accept me as a respectable woman. Have you thought of that?"

He was off the bed in an instant. "Gloria, I want to stay here. I want you to consider staying to share your life with me. You must know that I don't care what the town thinks, only what you think. I've fought people's opinions of me all my life. I'm half Comanche and am proud of that part of my past. But here, in this town, no one treats me different because of it." He wrapped his arms around her waist, pulled her to him and, inch by inch, lowered his mouth to hers. He moved his lips over hers then down her neck before returning to stare into her eyes. "It could be that way for you, for us. Tell me you'll consider a life with me here, in Fire Mountain."

She looked into his eyes. These were the eyes she wanted to look into the rest of her life. "All right, Sam. If you believe it's possible, I'll think about it."

Chapter Thirteen

A few weeks had passed since first learning of Victoria's possible duplicity when Sam showed Jamie another telegram from a judge in San Francisco. This one stated that Victoria was to be taken into immediate custody pending further investigation. She was to be held in the local jail until further instructions were received. "Looks like you don't have a choice, Sam," Jamie said as dispassionately as he could. "The sheriff is due back from Phoenix in a few days. Maybe he'll have some other ideas, but for now I don't see how you can avoid it."

Jamie knew Anna and Hen would be devastated and no doubt blame him. He didn't believe Victoria could hate him any more than she already did, but there wasn't a real choice. The order was clear. Sam had to arrest her, but at least they weren't asking that she be taken to California, yet.

"Do you want me to go with you?"

"No, Jamie. I'd better do this alone. Maybe you could keep an eye on the jail until I return. I arrested Ned Parker last night and he's still sleeping it off. His wife should be here anytime to take him home. His gun is in the drawer." Sam had resigned himself to the task, knowing it was futile to ignore a message such as this one.

Sam grabbed his hat, adjusted his gun belt, and picked up the handcuffs from a drawer.

"Do you really think those are necessary, Sam?" Even to Jamie the handcuffs seemed a little excessive.

"Thought I'd take the wagon so I wouldn't have to march Mrs. Wicklin through town. If I think it's needed, I'll cuff her to the wagon until we reach the jail." Sam knew the Wrights weren't the only ones who would be upset by the arrest. He expected half the town would be on his doorstep demanding an explanation, as well as her release. He also knew that Gloria would be among those demanding that Victoria be freed. Gloria's feelings on the matter ran high, and although she could usually be counted on to keep things professional, he thought she might very well cut him out of her life over this. He was reconciled to the town hating him. He just didn't know if he could get over losing Gloria.

While Sam headed to the livery to get the wagon, Jamie grabbed the letters and telegrams concerning Victoria and began to re-read them. He found paper and pencil and started jotting down questions as he read each several times. They were a place to start as well as a way to keep his mind off her. He and Sam had done all they could by telegram. Now they might need to step up their efforts, or at least he figured he'd have to increase his. Jamie didn't know how much more Sam could do as the town deputy. He was sworn to enforce the law, not investigate possible crimes outside of

Fire Mountain. But Jamie was a U.S. Marshal. He had no such restrictions.

He continued to focus on the task of reviewing everything they knew. He hoped Nell Parker would arrive soon so that he could leave before Sam returned. The last person Victoria would want to see when she entered the jail was Jamie MacLaren.

******

"There is nothing I can do, Mr. Wright. The warrant is legitimate, from a judge in San Francisco," Sam tried to explain.

"A judge who doesn't know Victoria and who didn't even ask her side of the story. It's not right, Hen. We can't let him take her. He and Jamie already believe she's guilty." Anna's voice was on the verge of breaking as she paced back and forth in the living room, trying to come to terms with her daughter's pending arrest.

"Now, Anna, we don't have a choice, and neither does Sam." Hen turned to Sam and pierced him with a look he gave very few people. "Do you believe Victoria is guilty, Sam? Does Jamie believe it?"

Sam ran his fingers through his hair and let out a breath before answering. "I just don't know. None of it makes sense to either Jamie or me, but the judge says there are witnesses and evidence. I haven't seen it, so I can't rightly answer either way." He stopped, deciding how best to proceed. "I do know that we'll do everything we can to hold off sending her back to San Francisco until we get

109

more information, either from them or on our own. I'm checking with Jerrod Minton regarding Victoria's rights, and we still need to hear from Mrs. Wallace's attorney. Jamie is sending a telegram to San Diego to get Tankard's story on record—he's the man who led Jamie to Hagan's ranch and rode with Hagan during the kidnapping. We'll do everything we can from this end."

"Thanks, Sam. We appreciate all your efforts. But you still didn't say if Jamie thinks she's guilty." Hen was determined to get an answer. They needed to know where they stood with Jamie.

"You'll have to ask him yourself..." Sam started to reply when he was cutoff.

"I can tell you what he believes." Victoria stood at the bottom of the stairs. She'd started packing a few things after Sam had arrived to announce the unwelcomed news. "He believes one-hundred-percent that I'm guilty. Besides that, he doesn't want to find any evidence that I'm innocent and being framed. He's getting the revenge he feels is due him. No, Jamie will be of no help to us." She placed her small bag on the floor then straightened and clasped her hands in front of her. "Do you plan to cuff me, Deputy Browning?"

"No, Mrs. Wicklin, not unless you force me to. But I do need to look in your bag before we leave."

"Of course. Help yourself," Victoria said with as steady a voice as she could muster.

Three minutes later they were boarding the wagon.

"Look, Mrs. Wicklin. I don't like the way this is playing out any more than you do. Nothing feels right about it. But you need to know that I'll do my job and I caution you not to do anything that makes me do something both of us will regret." Sam's gut told him this was all wrong, but he had taken an oath as a deputy, and as a marshal before that. He'd do his job whether his prisoner was a potentially innocent woman or an avowed bank robber. Made no difference. But he'd keep her safe while she was in his custody.

Victoria stiffened in her seat at his words, but nodded her understanding and stared straight ahead.

The trip to the jail only took five minutes but it felt much longer. As they drove down Main Street, people began filing out of businesses and houses to watch. Not many, but enough that the news would be all over town within the hour. As the wagon passed the Desert Dove, Gloria walked out through the double doors and locked her eyes onto Sam's. They were hard, devoid of emotion, and that one look gave him the answer he feared. No matter what happened now, he and Gloria might never work through their differences. Sometimes he hated his job.

Sam pulled the wagon to a stop in front of the jail, then helped Victoria down. Nell must be picking up Ned from the jail, as their wagon was on the other side of the street. He had hoped they'd be gone, and Jamie, too, but that wasn't meant to be.

Chapter Fourteen

Sam opened the door and motioned for Victoria to enter first. She started to follow his lead but stopped abruptly when she saw who was standing by the desk.

"Here to gloat, Marshal?" Victoria said with as much pride as she could muster while glaring into stone cold eyes.

Jamie winced at her words, but said nothing, just continued to help Ned outside to his wagon. At least Nell said nothing about Victoria. Her focus was on her still somewhat inebriated husband.

By the time he returned, Sam had secured Victoria in the farthest cell from the front. At least she'd have some privacy. Most of the cells had bars on three sides, which prevented prisoners from concealing items. This one was at the far end, with bars only in the front and a solid wall between it and the adjoining cell. The other cells were sparse, but this one had a small desk and chair as well as the standard cot. There were no drawers to stash her belongings, but at least she had a bag to hold her clothing, books, pen, and paper. There was an outhouse behind the jail that she could use, and fresh water was provided three times a day.

Jamie walked to the back and took in the cell. His gut clenched. Is this what he wanted? Did he still believe she deserved to be punished for the pain she'd caused him all those years ago? She looked so small standing alone, looking up at the only window, which was too high to see anything but the clear blue sky outside.

She must have sensed his presence. She turned and stared directly at him. "Deputy Browning?"

"What can I do for you, Mrs. Wicklin?"

"Is the marshal required to be here?" To her own surprise, Victoria's voice was steady and strong.

"No, Mrs. Wicklin, he's not required to be here. If the marshal's presence upsets you, I'll have him leave."

"He doesn't upset me, deputy. His presence is insignificant, really. But I'd prefer to be left alone." She turned her back on Jamie and pretended to assess her new living quarters. She didn't know how long she could keep her composure with Jamie watching her. It was hard being arrested for something she hadn't done, but so much harder to know the man she loved believed her to be guilty.

Jamie didn't budge. He just stood there, staring at her back, his gut twisting and his emotions in disarray. The truth slammed into him. He still loved her. Had always loved her. "I know you won't believe me, Torie, but I'm sorry. Sorry it came to this. More than anything, I regret that you think I want you here, in jail. That's not what I want. Not even close." He stopped, not wanting to say too much. "Don't blame Sam. He had no choice."

She said nothing. Just stood with her back to him and stared at a blank wall.

He finally realized she had no intention of answering or absolving him of guilt. He walked back to the desk. While Sam was at the Wright's, a letter from Mrs. Wallace's attorney, Silas Dunsford, had arrived. He decided to focus on it. The message was very clear. Hamilton Wicklin had somehow discovered the terms of the will, but Victoria had never been told about them. If what the lawyer said was true, the motivation to kill her husband, at least for the money, didn't exist. The attorney was adamant that Victoria could not, in any way, be involved in an attempt on Wicklin's life.

Jamie recalled that Torie insisted she was innocent of any involvement, but her protests had fallen on deaf ears. Both he and Sam had ignored her. Now she was in jail and blamed them for it.

"What's this?" Sam held up the letter as Jamie took a seat at the other desk.

"From her lawyer. It arrived while you were at the Wrights."

"A pretty good start," Sam offered. "Any word from the sheriff in San Diego?"

"He says Tankard's not talking. Told the sheriff that Hagan would kill him if he spoke to any lawman." Jamie's voice was flat as he relayed the news. He hadn't been surprised when the message arrived and he knew Tankard's lips would stay sealed.

114

Sam walked over to a small stove and poured a cup of coffee. "You want some?" Without waiting for a response, Sam got a second cup for Jamie and sat down. "Jerrod's coming by in the morning to talk with Victoria and review what we know so far. He's agreed to represent her, if needed." Jerrod Minton was considered the best attorney in the northern part of the territory and represented most of the ranchers.

"Good. That's real good," Jamie said idly as he sipped the hot brew and reviewed the events of the past couple of weeks.

"Sheriff Rawlins is due back tomorrow. You know he'll have some ideas about this mess." Sam cast a questioning look at Jamie.

"I'm sure he will. But I'm thinking it would clear up a lot of questions if Hagan could be brought in. He's the man with the answers as far as I can see, him and the attorney handling the will." Jamie paused. There was so much they didn't know. "Also, we need to find out anything we can about Wicklin. His finances, debts, and connections. Maybe that information will lead us to the truth."

"Best way to do all that is to hire someone we can trust, who understands San Francisco and knows how to ask around without tipping off Wicklin." Sam's voice trailed off as he went through his numerous contacts. "An ex-Pinkerton man would have the skills. I've worked with some who were good men, but others who were just as crooked as the men they pursued," Sam added as he searched his mind for possibilities. "Got it." Sam rose and walked toward the door. "Jefferson Delaney. You remember him, Jamie. He left the Marshals Service to join the Pinkertons. Wanted to move to the west coast and ended up in San Francisco. Think he's still there, but heard he isn't with the Pinkertons anymore. I'm going to find out." Sam grabbed his hat and headed toward the telegraph office, slamming the door behind him.

"Deputy, may I see you a minute?" Victoria called from the back. She must have thought Jamie had left when she heard the door slam. Jamie stood and strolled to the back.

"What can I do for you, Mrs. Wicklin?"

She looked up but stayed silent, shook her head, and turned away from him.

"You know you'll have to talk to me sometime, Torie."

"And why would that be, Marshal?"

"Well, for one thing, I need as much information from you as I can get to figure a way to discount Wicklin's accusations."

A skeptical sound escaped Victoria's lips. "Just stop, Jamie. We both know your true feelings for me no matter what you said earlier. You'd enjoy nothing more than to see me destroyed." She paused a moment before continuing. "Well, I won't discuss my marriage, the will, the kidnapping, nothing. It would've been better if you'd never found me. I had already escaped and would've made it back to San Francisco somehow." Her words faltered. She was on the verge of cracking but still held tight to the illusion of composure. "It would've been better if you hadn't come to my parent's house that night, if we hadn't walked to the knoll, if we hadn't ...," Tears glistened in her eyes, but she refused to break down in front of him.

Jamie stiffened as the words poured from Victoria. *Did he wish her destroyed?* He searched his heart but already knew that wasn't what he sought. What he'd wanted, at least for the first few years after her marriage, was to understand why she'd thrown away their future. The pain he'd felt had been crippling, but he'd pushed through it and made a life for himself without her. Seeing Victoria again brought back all the bad memories, but he had no wish to see her suffer as she was suffering now.

As far as her remarks about the walk to the knoll, he knew that was just her way of lashing out. She'd been as affected as him by their kisses. He knew her passionate response to him was genuine, but he'd broken it off, and for good reason. Neither had been ready to face the past or discuss the future. Now her future was uncertain and she was scared. What she needed was someone to lean on, talk with, trust, but it wasn't going to be him.

"Hey, Jamie, you still here?" Sam had returned. Jamie had hoped to have more time with Torie, but it wasn't to be.

"In the back. Be right out," Jamie turned back to Victoria. "All right, Torie. For now I'll leave you alone. But there'll be a time when we'll talk. Don't doubt that. And not just about what's happening now, but about the past."

******

It had been several days with no further word from the aunt's attorney, and nothing at all from the judge who'd issued the warrant. Although Sam had located the ex-Pinkerton man, Jefferson Delaney, he'd received no new information about Wicklin. The lack of communication frustrated both Sam and Jamie, but Sheriff Rawlins seemed to take it as good news. At least they weren't looking at sending her to California right away, which gave them time to continue their own investigation.

The one disturbing bit of news was from the sheriff in San Diego. Billy Tankard had escaped, with help from Miguel Hagan. The sheriff and his deputies had found the ranch using Jamie's directions, but it was already deserted. Jamie doubted that Hagan had any interest in finding Victoria, but it was something that niggled at the back of his mind, and those were warnings that Jamie rarely ignored.

"If we don't hear anything from Delaney by tomorrow, I'll send another telegram," Sam said as he and Jamie sat at their table in Mattie's restaurant. "I suppose I should try the attorney once more, too. See if he's back from Boston."

"You know there's a possibility that Hagan may be on his way here to find Victoria. Tankard said the man never forgives a slight and he's one

118

mean bastard. Not many are as cruel or vindictive as he is." Jamie couldn't shake the feeling that something bad was about to happen. His instincts had saved him on many occasions and his gut told him to prepare for trouble.

"What do you think we should do? You know the sheriff thinks you're over-reacting, that there's no way Hagan will draw attention to himself by coming here. But me, I respect your concerns." Sam had known Jamie long enough to take his friend's unease about Billy's escape seriously.

"Not much except be watchful. Better to concentrate on getting information that will help us release Victoria than worry about Hagan. I just don't like it, that's all." Jamie stood to leave. "See you later, Sam. I need to go speak with someone about a favor."

Chapter Fifteen

"I don't know, Jamie. There must be someone else she'd open up to faster than me." Gloria stood at the end of the long bar with Jamie's arm around her, as he tried to persuade her to visit Victoria.

"She needs a friend, Gloria. Someone she can talk with who has no association whatsoever with Sam, her family, or me. Someone she feels she can trust, which I guarantee isn't me right now."

Sam, she thought. Gloria hated the way he'd looked at her when she'd walked outside to watch him take Mrs. Wicklin to jail. Yes, she'd been angry that he was the one who had arrested Victoria, but she knew it was his job. It had been almost a week—six days and nights—and no sign of him. She thought they'd started something together. They'd spoken of marriage.

Sam was different. He accepted what she was, her past, but also her dreams to sell out and start a new life. They'd talked so much over the past few months that they'd become good friends long before she had accepted him into her bed. Then there was the situation with Victoria, and just like that, it seemed he wanted no part of her. She supposed Jamie's words—that she had no association with Sam—were accurate.

"All right, Jamie. I'll do what I can, but as a friend, not because I plan to pump her for information and pass it along to you. If she does tell me something that would help, I'll let you know."

Just then, Jamie and Gloria became aware of Sam standing behind them. Jamie dropped his arm from around Gloria and turned toward the deputy.

"Sam. Just the man I want to talk to." Jamie hadn't shared his idea with anyone but Gloria, but now that she had agreed, he needed to confide in his friend.

"That a fact." Sam glanced past Jamie to Gloria. Their eyes locked but neither said a word. His face was like granite, eyes cold, piercing her with an unspoken accusation.

"Uh, yea." Jamie looked at Sam, then at Gloria. Something was going on here but damned if he knew what it was. "Victoria won't speak with you or me, and talks only briefly with her folks. She needs to talk to someone, and you know how good Gloria is at getting people to trust her. Talk to her."

"Yea, I do know that." Sam was still staring at Gloria. To her credit, her eyes never wavered, but held his in a silent challenge.

"Well, Gloria's offered to visit Victoria regularly, try to get her to open up a little. If nothing else, Victoria will have another woman she can talk to who isn't connected to you or me." There was another meaningful glance between Sam and Gloria, but Jamie let it go and continued. "She's going crazy in that cell, with only you and the sheriff around. Maybe she'll tell Gloria things that could help us."

"You mean help us convict her, Jamie, or help us free her?" Sam was still fuming from the sight of Jamie wrapped around Gloria. She hadn't waited long to find someone to replace him.

"Look, Sam, I understand that most everyone doubts my motives. Hell, I've doubted them myself." He looked first at Sam, then at Gloria. "My concern right now is to discover the truth. If there's something else on your mind, if I'm missing something, you better tell me now."

Sam and Gloria finally broke eye contact to focus on Jamie's idea.

"Fine, Jamie. Let's go ahead with it. Gloria can come by anytime she wants as long as someone else is there." Sam downed the drink that Jamie had set in front of him and left the bar. Gloria just stared at the empty space he left behind and felt more alone than she had in a long, long time.

******

"Silas, I heard you were back in town. How was your trip east?" Hamilton Wicklin walked into the attorney's office unannounced, but that wasn't unusual.

Silas Dunsford closed the file he'd been reviewing before looking up. This was the one person he hadn't wanted to see on his first day back. Bea had been right to cut him out of her will. He was a philanderer and a cheat, two things Silas didn't abide, and neither had his client. She'd worked with Silas to hammer out the details of her will so that Ham couldn't directly touch a cent from the estate. He would be cared for, assuming he and Victoria stayed married after the seven years were up, but he'd inherit nothing. Not ever.

"Hamilton. What brings you here today?" Silas' words were brusque. He'd already guessed it was about the man's wife. The seven years were up and Victoria's husband knew that Silas was now obligated to share the details of Bea's will with her. News of her rescue had reached them, and now she was free to divorce and enjoy the estate that Bea had left, without any further obligations to Wicklin. Her arrest would be a complication, but Silas knew there wasn't a chance the woman was guilty of Hamilton's charges. Charges, Silas suspected, that were fabricated to gain Wicklin what he really wanted—his aunt's estate.

"Let's just say I want to know your plans for telling Victoria about the inheritance. She's in jail you know. Tried to have me killed. But, as you can see, her plan failed."

Silas wanted to wipe the smirk off Hamilton's face, but propriety and age won out over emotions.

"Well now, Hamilton, hard to see how she could have planned your death while being held hostage by that Hagan fella. Doesn't add up to me." Silas picked up the folder and placed it inside his safe, locked it, and turned back to Wicklin. "Course, doesn't help you either way. If she did as you say and was found guilty, everything of Bea's goes to the charities your aunt designated. Still won't go to you. Seems to me your chances are better if you get her back to the city and make amends for all the—shall we say, unfortunate?—things you did to her."

Wicklin's already ruddy complexion turned beet red at this news. Although he'd managed to obtain information from the pretty and very accommodating secretary Silas had employed several years back, she'd only supplied information about how the annual allowance, house, and restaurant were to be handled. He'd also learned of the clause about staying married for at least seven years before the entire estate would be released. She'd said nothing more. He hadn't thought to ask if there were other provisions. Wicklin assumed that upon Victoria's death all would pass to him.

"Guess you didn't know that bit of information." The attorney watched the man's reaction. "None of it will ever go to you. Your aunt's wishes were very clear and she made sure the will reflected them. If your wife stays married to you for seven years, she gets it all. If she dies or leaves you before the seven years are up, then it will all go to the charities. Pretty simple and clear. Victoria's as bright as they come, Hamilton, and, as far as I can tell, fair also. I doubt she'd cut you out completely. But she might if you keep up with this story about plotting your murder. You really expect people to believe such hogwash?" Silas had no use for Hamilton and wanted him out of his office and, preferably, out of San Francisco and Victoria's life.

"That woman tried to kill me and I'll prove it. After that, I'll hire the best attorney in the area and tear my aunt's will apart," Wicklin fumed as he placed both hands on Silas's desk and leaned forward. "And you'd be better off just staying out of my way."

"Is that a threat, Wicklin?"

"Just fair warning, Dunsford. No one, and that includes you, is going to stop me from getting what should've been mine in the first place." He stalked to the door and walked out.

Silas lowered himself into the chair, sat back, and started thinking. As he saw it, there were several things he had to take care of right away, and the first was a letter to the sheriff in Fire Mountain.

Chapter Sixteen

Gloria wondered if he'd even acknowledge her when she entered the jail. Several days had passed since Sam had been in the saloon. Either he'd not returned, or she'd been in her office when he was there. She suspected the first, as Ross would've mentioned it to her if the deputy had come around. Sam had been at the jail when she'd visited Victoria, but he'd ignored her, merely motioning for her to head to the back cell.

She'd stopped by the jail twice daily, with dinner at midday, and again with supper in the evening. It was something she'd wanted to do, and the invitation from Jamie had been the nudge she needed. Victoria was cool at first, but as the days passed, she'd opened up a little. The fact was, Gloria liked her. She knew that becoming friends with a woman outside the saloon would be too much to ask, but she hoped that once exonerated, Victoria would acknowledge her from time to time. That was more than Sam was willing to do.

"Deputy," Gloria pushed open the door and stepped inside. He just nodded. *God, why does he always have to look so good*? Gloria thought as she passed by his desk on her way to the back. She asked herself for the hundredth time what had happened to cause them to act like strangers, barely acknowledging each other. What had she done to ruin something with a man who was very special? The man she loved?

Sam watched Gloria walk past him to visit Victoria. He just couldn't get her out of his mind. She haunted him day and night. Having her come by the jail twice a day, spend time here, and not even look at him was like salt in a wound. Didn't she understand that he had a job to do? He didn't want Victoria to be found guilty of the charges any more than Gloria did, but his hands were tied.

He supposed it didn't really matter. It appeared to Sam like she'd already moved on to another MacLaren. His stomach clenched at the thought of the two of them together. He knew Jamie was still in love with Victoria, but Gloria was a beautiful woman, and Sam doubted few men could refuse her if she provided encouragement. Truth was, he'd never seen her encourage anyone, except him. Hell, he hadn't even told Jamie anything about his feelings for Gloria since his friend was so wrapped up in the situation with their prisoner. So many other things had happened that he'd just never gotten around to it. Sam knew Jamie would never take up with a friend's woman if he knew about it, but now it may be too late.

"Hello, Victoria." Gloria laid the basket down and waited for Sam to come back, open the cell door, and pass the food to Victoria. Next, he'd lock the cell and walk back to his desk. The same routine every time she came by.

"Gloria. It's good to see you again. I hope this isn't too much of an inconvenience. I know you're busy." Although sincere, Victoria's voice was resigned and tinged with despair.

"Don't be silly. This is the best part of my day. You have to understand that I'm around men all day, everyday, who are surly, raucous, or just plan ornery, and usually drunk. Or, I have the company of the women who work for me. Since I'm the boss, they don't come to me much just to talk. But my time with you is different. It's my time." Gloria's words were true. She wished she could somehow tuck these times with Victoria away so that they could be taken out and revisited in the future, when she returned to her solitary routine. She had a good life compared to many women, and she knew it, but this time with Victoria had become very special.

"Oh, fried chicken," Victoria exclaimed as she opened the basket and peered in, "and pie. Even if the accommodations aren't great, the food certainly is."

"Eat, Victoria. Don't wait. I know you must be hungry." Gloria smiled as Victoria lifted a piece of chicken out of the basket and took a bite.

"So, where were we? Oh, yes. I'd just gotten into town and started working for Clive at the Desert Dove. Jamie had asked you to marry him, right?"

Victoria nodded at Gloria's summary of their last conversation. She had shared more than she'd planned, but last night she'd felt tired and sorry for herself.

Victoria swallowed some chicken and took a drink of water from the cup Sam had given her earlier. "Was it hard, Gloria?" At Gloria's puzzled expression, she explained. "You know. Being with men you didn't know? You were so young."

Gloria thought back to those days and how frightened she'd been. She was from a wealthy family in New Orleans. Her father was a harsh man and had planned for her to marry a much older gentleman so that two family fortunes could be combined. Gloria had rebelled and refused her father's request. Instead of reacting as she'd anticipated, he threw her out of the house with little more than a few clothes and a little money. He'd called her a whore's daughter and told her to never return. She hadn't. She had only been sixteen.

"Well, yes, it was hard. But you have to understand no one would hire me. I tried to get work in all kinds of places. At a laundry, as a seamstress' apprentice, washing dishes, scrubbing floors. I would've taken anything, but no one would hire me. My father had told everyone that I was a whore like my mother and threatened anyone who was inclined to hire me." Gloria's words stopped abruptly as she recalled the day she had been told, by one of the more respected women in town, that her mother had taken a lover a year before Gloria was born. Even though her mother denied it, her father believed Gloria was not his, but the child of another man. After that she understood her father's anger, but she'd never learned the truth of her heritage.

"Gloria? Are you okay? You don't have to say anymore if you don't want to." Victoria's eyes were filled with compassion.

"No, it's all right. I was just remembering the first time I was with a man. He must've been about twenty-three. He was very handsome, and looking back, very gentle. I'd just started and was scared to death. By then I was in Abilene. An older woman took me in and told me what to expect. Then she made sure my first time was with someone she approved. He asked me if I was sure this was what I wanted. When I told him I really had no choice, he nodded and started to undress me. He took his time, made me feel special, not dirty like you'd think." In her mind, Gloria could still remember the young cowboy who took her. He'd been in town looking for his older brother who'd been missing since the war. She knew it was only for one night, but she'd still felt the sting when he walked out the door and never returned. She'd cried the rest of the night. Gloria never even knew his name.

"After that it became a little easier, even if it never meant a thing. It was a job and it kept me alive. I made my way to Arizona and Fire Mountain. Seemed like forever, but I was here by the time I was nineteen. Clive hired me right away. We always worked well together. I never mouthed back at him and never tried to cheat him out of his cut. When he decided to move on, we worked out an arrangement so that I could buy the saloon.

Best deal I ever made." Gloria stopped short of saying that at the time, she was seeing Jamie's brother, Niall. Perhaps Victoria already knew about it.

"You are so independent, Gloria. I envy you the ability to make your own decisions and not be controlled by a man." Victoria's voice had turned bitter and there was pain in her eyes.

Gloria hesitated. She didn't want to push but there'd be no better time. "What happened, Victoria? Why'd you change your mind about marrying Jamie?" They were at a juncture. Either Victoria trusted Gloria enough to tell her or she didn't.

Victoria dropped her head into her hands then rubbed her eyes and stood up from the chair where she'd been sitting. She paced to the window and gazed up to the opening, which started six feet above the cell floor. Gloria didn't think she'd respond.

"Jamie left town with his brothers. They were moving the herd to sell so we knew he'd be gone about two weeks. He'd just asked me to marry him. Of course, I said yes." She stopped a moment, remembering that day on the knoll. *I love you, Torie. Marry me.* Jamie's words still had the ability to make her smile while at the same time cause intense heartache. "It was right after he left that a stranger, Hamilton Wicklin, came to town. But he wasn't a stranger, at least not to my parents. They'd been friends with his aunt for years. She wanted them to agree to a marriage between me and her nephew, to connect the families, but they knew I loved Jamie and planned to marry him. My parents always liked Jamie and wanted me to be happy. We told Hamilton that I was already betrothed. He appeared to take the news fine, but asked if he and I could at least get to know each other while he was in town."

Victoria stopped as if remembering something very painful before she continued. "He was handsome, suave, and I guess," she closed her eyes, trying to think, "worldly would be the word I'd choose. At least I thought he was at the time. Even though Papa objected, Mama thought it was fine for us to spend some time together. He began coming by each day to visit." Victoria paused, but didn't continue for several minutes. Gloria was quiet, believing if she were patient, Victoria would continue. She did.

"One afternoon he asked if I would meet him at the livery that evening and give him my opinion on a horse he wanted to buy. I was young and flattered at his request. It never occurred to me there was something strange in his invitation. I met him that night, but instead of looking at a horse, he cornered me, forced himself on me. I fought as best I could, hitting his face, pushing and kicking, but he was too big, and strong. He was rough and it hurt a great deal. Afterwards, I just laid on the floor of the livery and cried."

She took a ragged breath and lowered herself onto the edge of the cot before continuing in a whisper. "He just stood there, looking down on me, laughing. He laughed, Gloria. What kind of man does that? Rapes a woman, then laughs?" She took another shuddering breath before continuing. "Hamilton informed me that we would marry, and if I refused, he'd spread the word that I'd come on to him. He was only taking what was offered," she said in a disgusted voice. "There were other threats, horrible threats that I believed he would carry out. I truly thought I had no choice."

Gloria was shocked at Victoria's confession. "My God, Victoria. What did your parents say?"

"I never told them." Victoria worked to control her breathing and rein in the anger that threatened to overwhelm her. "You must understand that his threats were very real to me. I didn't think I had a choice. I told Mama and Papa that I'd changed my mind about Jamie and wished to marry Hamilton. We argued, but in the end, they accepted my decision. Oh, Gloria, it was horrible."

"And no one else ever knew the truth?"

"Only his Aunt Beatrice, and she guessed. She knew how callous Ham could be. Bea once told me that he'd always been cruel and self-absorbed. That's why she asked if I would be willing to handle the annual funds that would be provided upon her death. Of course I said yes but never thought she'd pass within a few short years." A tear made its way down her cheek. She swiped it away with her hand, then looked up at Gloria. "I grew to love Aunt Bea very much over the time I knew her. I never understood how Hamilton could've become the person he did with her as his guardian."

The two women sat in silence for a long time, each lost in their own thoughts, both thinking of the other and the broken dreams and sorrows each had endured to make it this far.

"Have the last few years been terribly hard, living with that bastard?" Gloria blushed at what she had called the other woman's husband, but Victoria just waived it off.

"Not as bad as you'd think, Gloria. I came to discover that he was not allowed back into his aunt's home unless he returned a married man with a suitable bride, preferably me. Apparently, he knew no other suitable women. His aunt's instructions to seek me out made his task easy." A bitter laugh escaped her lips. "After that first time, at the livery, he came to me so seldom I could count them on two hands. He was always drunk and angry when he'd seek me out. It was as if others had turned him down and he'd take their rejection out on me. I dealt with it in my own way. I found it wasn't too bad if I just laid there and let him do what he wanted." She smiled at the thought. "You see, it would make him even more angry if I just laid unmoving. When he was drunk and angry he was unable to—well, you know," and gestured in a small circle with her hand. Then she started laughing. It was a small giggle at first that grew into a full, stomach-churning laugh, which caused tears to come to her eyes. Before they knew it, Gloria was holding her side, laughing just as hard.

"What in tarnation is going on back there?" Sam yelled from the front office.

They looked at each other, but his question just caused them to laugh more.

Gloria wiped tears from her cheeks then looked up to see Sam standing over her with his fists on his hips and a confounded look on his face. "Will someone tell what is going on here?" he asked again in a somewhat calmer voice.

"Oh, Sam," Gloria said as another laughed escaped. "Sorry. But you just wouldn't understand." She winked at Victoria and stood. She didn't want to leave, but she still had to work on the books and get an order ready for their supplier in Phoenix. Besides, she knew she'd be back in a few hours.

Chapter Seventeen

They were close. Miguel and his men had ridden for days, had asked a lot of questions, and everything pointed to MacLaren taking Mrs. Wicklin to Fire Mountain. Billy had been right when he guessed she wouldn't return to San Francisco right away. He'd overheard the sheriff in San Diego mention she wanted to see her family, her real family, not her husband. That was fine with Miguel, as he knew Wicklin was dead. Lying at the bottom of the bay.

Hagan had plans for MacLaren and unfinished business with Victoria Wicklin. She was his and she'd been taken from him. It didn't matter that she'd tried to run. What belonged to him always belonged to him. He'd find her and make his claim very clear.

"We will camp here tonight, Hector. You will ride into this Fire Mountain. Find her and come back to make plans, si? Do not drink. You must have a clear head. Do you understand, mi amigo?"

"Si, Miguel, I will do as you ask. But..." Hector's words trailed off.

"What is it you wish to say?" Miguel allowed no arguments from his men. Seldom did they question him or comment on his orders.

"The woman. We would like her when you are finished with her. It is only fair, si, Miguel?"

Miguel just laughed. "Ah, you want to share what is mine? I will think on this. Maybe. When I am done with her I will decide if I will share her. We must find her first, si?" He had no intention of ever sharing this woman. She would belong only to him.

******

"What's it say, Sam?" Sheriff Rawlins asked. They'd just received information from Jefferson Delaney on what he'd learned.

"As we suspected, Wicklin's unscrupulous and corrupt, but also smart, with friends everywhere. Has a Judge in his pocket as well as the local constable. Silas Dunsford, Mrs. Wallace's attorney, is in the hospital. Someone broke into his office, beat him, left him for dead, and may have stolen some papers. Everything was torn up. But Dunsford didn't die. Delaney hired a couple of his associates to keep watch on the attorney, just in case his attacker reappears to finish the job. He's working with the attorney's assistant to identify what, if anything, was taken. Jefferson will be back in touch soon." Sam placed the message on Rawlins' desk, looked around the office, then motioned his head in the direction of the back cells. "What now, Sheriff?"

"We keep gathering evidence. We can't let her go yet, but Jerrod is working with Judge Kinsdale. He'll get back to us as soon as they review all the information. Kinsdale knows of the judge in San Francisco. Heard nothing good about him. But, he is powerful, at least in that area. We need to be careful how we proceed." Rawlins was a longtime friend of the Wright's, a fair man who was determined to clear Victoria, but he wanted it done right.

"Agreed," Sam said as he poked his head around to check on Victoria. "Anyone brought Mrs. Wicklin's dinner today, Sheriff?" Sam had been out of the office the last two days investigating reports of cattle thefts, leaving the office to Rawlins.

"Not yet. Expect Gloria anytime. You want to grab dinner first?" Joe Rawlins was aware of the situation that had developed between Gloria and his deputy. Fact was, a couple of the leading citizens, both female, couldn't wait to tell him what they'd heard about the town deputy taking up with the saloon owner. Joe couldn't care less, but also didn't want Sam's private life interfering with his duties.

"Uh, no. Why don't you go ahead? I'll eat later." Sam took his hat off and placed it on the rack next to the door, then settled behind his desk. Damn, he missed seeing Gloria, being with her. Even though she hadn't spared him a glance, just seeing her each day was worth the discomfort it caused. She could make him hard with just a look.

The more he thought about it, the less he believed she'd taken up with Jamie. It just didn't make sense. Gloria had always been honest with him. She'd been with only two men in her life by choice. Niall MacLaren and him. After Niall remarried, she hadn't been with anyone else until

Sam. Not knowing for certain was driving him crazy. Well, there was only one way to find out. Ask her.

******

Another hour ticked by before the door opened, announcing Gloria's arrival. She carried the usual basket, but this time also had a small sack.

She looked at Sam while walking towards the back.

"Got to see what you have in the sack, Gloria." The words came out harsh, not what Sam intended.

She glared at him but opened the bag. All he saw were some clean clothes for Victoria, another book, and some cards. Cards?

"Planning to corrupt our guest?" Sam asked as he held up the cards and attempted a smile.

"Don't be ridiculous, Deputy. She's bored and wants to learn how to play poker. No betting, just points. That okay with you, Deputy, or does it break your rules?"

This wasn't going as Sam had hoped. He wanted to talk to her, find out if she still had any feelings for him at all.

"Go ahead, Gloria. But I'd like a few words with you, in private, before you leave." Their eyes locked for a few seconds before Gloria nodded and broke contact.

Gloria wondered what Sam was up to as she made her way to Victoria's cell. He hadn't said ten civil words to her in days and now he wanted a conversation. Probably wanted to find out if she'd learned anything useful from Victoria. She'd learned a lot about his prisoner, but nothing she felt would help the case, and nothing she would share with him.

Gloria had returned with supper the day she'd told of her life since New Orleans and Victoria had shared her encounter with Wicklin. She found that Victoria was eager to learn more about her. Victoria's friends apparently numbered as few as her own.

Gloria had admitted her love for Sam. It was good to get it out, even if it wasn't to Sam himself. She confided in Victoria that they'd discussed marriage but that he'd rejected her not long after their affair began. The rejection had stung. She suspected it was her profession. He must've realized there was no future in law if he was saddled with someone who'd made her living the way she had before becoming a saloon owner.

Victoria disagreed. She didn't know Sam well, but he seemed to be an honorable man, not one to lead Gloria on, then dump her without a thought. Victoria encouraged her to confront Sam, learn the truth.

Gloria wanted Sam and hoped he still felt the same, but her gut told her otherwise. If his desire for her was still strong he would have come to her by now, but he hadn't.

Victoria spoke more freely of the difficult years with Wicklin. Of his open affairs, even bringing women to their home, into his room. His harsh treatment of her and open hostility when he'd be forced to come to her for more money were the most difficult. Ham made threats, saying if she kept denying him the funds he demanded, he'd make her life a continuous nightmare. Victoria knew he spoke the truth.

But most significantly, at least in Gloria's mind, was Victoria admitting that she was still in love with Jamie. Had been all these years. There would never be another man for her. Once she was cleared of the charges and her divorce was final, she planned to return to San Francisco. She couldn't stay in the same town as Jamie and pretend she didn't care. Gloria sighed. If Victoria left, Gloria would lose her only female friend. She lifted her chin and put a smile on her face as she entered the cell.

"Hello, Victoria. Brought you some stew and biscuits this time. Real good, too. Hope you're hungry."

Victoria looked up and smiled. "Hello, Gloria." She sat at her small desk. "Just getting a letter ready for Attorney Dunsford. He needs to check on the house and servants. I told him I hope to be home soon."

She must be unaware, Gloria thought, that Silas Dunsford was brutally attacked and, as far as they knew, was still in the hospital.

"I'll give it to Sam on the way out." Gloria smiled as she held out her hand for the letter.

"Speaking of Sam, have you spoken with him yet?"

"No, not yet, but he wants to speak with me before I leave. Must be about the saloon." At least she hoped it was something like that and not about trying to get her to talk about her friend, his prisoner.

"Well, that may be your chance. The way I see it, you don't have much to lose."

"Oh, Victoria," Gloria sighed and dropped her head in her hands. "I have everything to lose if he confirms what I suspect."

******

"You wanted to speak with me?" Gloria walked up to where Sam sat reading over another telegram.

"Um, yes. If you have a few minutes." His voice was quiet, he wouldn't look at her, and his hands fidgeted with the pencil they held. Her heart sank, and in that instant she knew what was coming.

"Look, Sam, if this is about you and me, and all the things we said, the plans we spoke of, I want you to know I won't hold you to them. Sometimes men say things they don't mean, change their mind, then want out." Her voice was deteriorating. She willed the tears that had formed in her eyes not to fall. She would not break down in front of him.

"Gloria," his voice was barely above a whisper and this time he did look up.

"No, Sam, it's all right. I know what you want to say and you don't need to. Please forget about our talks on sharing a life. I'd never hold you to it. The last days have shown me that a life here, with me, is something you don't truly want. I understand." She didn't realized that Sam had been staring at her as she tried to accept what she thought would be his rejection. "I should get back to the saloon now." She turned her back to him, walking for the door.

"I love you."

His words stopped her, but she still couldn't look at him. She was too afraid to hope that she'd heard him right, or his words were true.

He moved behind her and placed his hands on her hips, drawing her back to him. "I love you, Gloria. I want you more than any woman I've ever known, and not just for now. I want you in my life always." He placed a kiss at the back of her neck and heard her moan. His hands moved around her waist to settle her against him as his lips worked their way down her neck to her shoulder, pushing away the shawl she wore.

"Sam, I thought..." she sighed as he continued to trail kisses along her shoulder. "I love you too," she murmured as another moan escaped. She turned to wrap her arms around his neck and take what she'd been wanting for much too long.

Chapter Eighteen

Sheriff Rawlins stood with his hands on his hips staring at the latest message from Jefferson Delaney.

"Sam, look at this."

Sam struggled to calm the thrill of what had happened with Gloria earlier that day. She loved him, and damned if he wasn't going to make the most of it.

"Sam?" the sheriff looked up at him questioningly.

"Sorry, what'd you say?"

Rawlins shook his head, but smiled, picked up the message and handed it to his deputy. "It's from Delaney. Take a look."

Sam read it twice before raising his eyes. "So the only item that seems to be missing from the attorney's office is the folder with all of Mrs. Wallace's legal documents. Interesting."

"That's my thought exactly," Rawlins nodded. "Dunsford is getting better and Delaney hopes he'll identify Wicklin as the assailant. He also has men searching Wicklin's home for the folder."

Sam shook his head. "Unless the guy is a complete idiot, I doubt they'll find it. Says Delany's got the information on the judge who issued the warrant." Sam smiled. "Seems the judge may be arrested for kickbacks from more than just

Wicklin. This may be the deal that seals all their fates."

Rawlins made no effort to hide his disdain. "You can bet if the judge is arrested, Wicklin won't be far behind, and Wicklin won't go down alone. He'll squeal on Hagan, and anyone else, to get a lighter sentence. I bet the witnesses against Victoria disappear as fast as they materialized."

Just as the sheriff sat back in his chair the jail door slammed open and a man neither Rawlins nor Sam had ever seen before, but recognized from numerous wanted posters, strolled into the room.

"What the hell is going on?" Rawlins boomed as he jumped from his desk.

"Ah, the sheriff. And the deputy, si?" The menace in the man's voice put both lawmen on alert.

"Hagan." It was all Rawlins had time to say. Miguel fired, the bullet catching the sheriff off guard. He fell to the floor, not moving. Sam started to reach for his gun.

"No, señor. I would not do that if I were you. Your sheriff, he may die this day, but you? No, you do not have to die. Unless, of course, that is your wish."

Glancing down at the wounded sheriff, Sam lowered his hand and let both arms hang at his sides. "What do you want, Hagan?"

"Ah, that is much better." The outlaw turned to motion in three men. Three more stayed outside to watch and guard their horses. "It is the woman I want. Who else? The lawman, MacLaren, took her from me. What is mine, I keep. You understand, señor?"

Hagan indicated for his men to watch Sam as he moved past him to the cells in back. "She is here, si?" He asked but already knew the answer. Hector had found the location of the woman without much effort. The whole town talked of her arrest.

Sam stood motionless. He expected Jamie at any time, and hoped his friend spotted Hagan's men before it was too late.

******

Jamie had left the ranch an hour earlier to meet with Sam and Rawlins. He was taking his time, enjoying the ride on Rebel, trying to clear his mind. He and Rebel had been together for years. Rebel had been born on the ranch, the foal of their uncle's stallion and their aunt's mare. Jamie had trained him. It was Rebel who had carried him away from Fire Mountain years before, after he and Niall had quarreled one too many times about Victoria. Now he rode his horse back into town to learn of news that might clear or convict her of murder.

He'd just passed the Dove when a shot rang out. His immediate response had him looking into the saloon to see what commotion had occurred on a Monday night, an odd night for mischief, but all seemed to be calm as he peered over the swinging door entry to the bar. Then he looked further down the street to the jail. Three men, all facing towards the street, and seven horses. His gut twisted as his eyes focused on the tack and he recognized gear used most often by Mexican riders. They hadn't seen him. Jamie turned Rebel into a side street, dismounted, grabbed his extra guns, and began to make his way down the back street behind the jail. He knew that what he saw did not bode well for Sam, Rawlins, or Victoria.

******

"Miguel." The words were spoken in a whisper, but Victoria felt panic at the sight of her former captor.

"Si, querida, I have come for you. Did you think I would not?" The sneer on his face sickened her. She heard the keys rattle in the lock and saw the door swing open. Miguel filled the space.

Instinctively she moved to the back of the cell, searching for anything she could get her hands on to hold him off. She wouldn't go with him. She'd die first.

"Ah, do not be afraid. You will go with me now, back to the ranch. We will finish what was started, si?"

"No, Miguel. I'll never go with you. Never let your filthy hands touch me again. I'll die first." Her voice sounded calm, but panic rolled over her.

Miguel's face turned red at her words and his eyes hardened. The gun he held in one hand now partnered with a knife that appeared in the other. "Perhaps we will not wait for the ranch. Perhaps I will take you now, here, in this gringo's jail."

"You lay a hand on her, Hagan, and I'll shoot it off." The words were cold, unwavering. She couldn't see him, but she knew Jamie's voice.

Hagan turned from Victoria. "Ah, you are MacLaren. You killed my men and you threaten me. That is a dangerous thing, señor. I take only what is mine. This woman belongs to me." The outlaw pivoted just enough to get a shot off, but didn't fire. A quick shot wouldn't be the vengeance Miguel wanted from the man who'd stolen Victoria from him. No. He planned to take MacLaren with him and kill him slowly, with the woman watching.

Jamie's jaw hardened at the words. The lawman knew just one of them would survive this night, and by God, it would be him. He wouldn't let the man take Victoria from him. She was his. No other man would ever have her again, except him. "I think not, Hagan. Now, drop the gun and knife before I'm forced to drop them for you."

******

The sound of voices in the back had all three of Hagan's men turning toward the cells. It was just the chance Sam needed. He fell behind the desk, drew his gun and before they knew what had happened, two men fell to the floor. The third pointed his gun at the desk, fired, and backed through the open door. Sam heard yelling from outside along with more gunfire, but no one else came into the jail. He paused briefly to check the sheriff. Rawlins was still breathing. Sam grabbed his kerchief and stuffed it around the wound

148

before getting to his feet to move toward the back cells.

******

Miguel's knife hand began to move, but at the sound of gunfire, his eyes flew toward the front office. Before the outlaw could focus back on MacLaren, Hagan felt pain and looked down to see blood soaking his shirt. The knife he'd been about to use dropped to the floor followed by the gun in his other hand. That split second was all Jamie needed to be sure he could get off a shot without endangering Victoria. Hagan took one last look at Victoria, then MacLaren, before dropping to one knee, then the other, and falling to his side, clutching his chest.

Jamie moved toward the outlaw, kneeling to check the wound. It was a clean shot. Miguel would not last long. "Why did you kill him, Miguel? Wicklin. Why kill him?"

Hagan coughed, blood spewing with the effort. "The woman, señor. I wanted his woman. She is mine."

"Did she ask you to kill him?" Jamie urged the man on before they lost him. But Miguel was laboring, his life oozing out of him as the blood flowed from his body. Jamie shook him slightly. "Miguel? Did Victoria ask you to kill Wicklin?"

The man coughed but turned his glazed eyes to the lawman. "No."

Jamie watched as Hagan took a last shuddering breath.

"So that's it." Sam stood behind his friend, glad he'd heard the outlaw's last words. He stared at Hagan and placed his hand on Jamie's shoulder. "I'm going for Doc Minton. Rawlins is out in front with a bullet wound in his shoulder. Don't think it's serious, but needs to be taken care of. You best take care of Victoria." Sam nodded toward the woman still standing at the back wall.

Jamie looked up. What he saw stopped him cold. Victoria stood flat against the back wall, her hand holding the only weapon she had, a writing pen, but it was positioned as a knife, ready to attack. Her face was contorted, her features set. She wouldn't have let Hagan take her alive. The thought sent chills through him.

He stood and walked forward, slow steps that wouldn't alarm her. "Torie. It's all right. He's dead. You can drop the pen now, it's over." His words penetrated and she looked up into soft grey eyes full of concern. She sagged against the wall, dropping her makeshift weapon.

Jamie reached out to catch her and place her on the cot. Victoria's glazed eyes didn't focus, but at least she was alive.

******

"You'll live," Doc Minton told the sheriff as he closed his bag and stood. "A couple more inches down to the right and I'd have another body on my hands. You'll have to take it easy awhile, but you're one lucky man, Joe."

150

"Thanks, doc. While you're here, maybe you could check on Victoria. She's a little shaken up. Just want to be sure he's okay. She's in back with MacLaren."

"Sure thing." Doc grabbed his satchel and walked to the back. "Victoria, Jamie, how you doing after all the commotion?" He sat on the cot and began to check her over.

"I'm fine." Victoria answered. The doctor's eyebrows arched up. "He never touched me. The man will never be able to hurt anyone again. It's over." She visibly relaxed as she realized the truth that flowed from her.

"Okay. And you, Jamie?" Doc turned toward the younger man.

"Fine." Jamie continued to watch Torie, concerned that she wasn't as calm as she seemed. "How's the sheriff?"

"He'll live. Too ornery to die, you know. He's already shouting orders about removing the bodies. Well, if that's it, I'd better get back to the office. Get the bodies ready to bury in the pauper's cemetery, right?"

"That's the truth of it, doc. Those men don't even deserve to be buried with the good people in that spot, but it's all there is. Thanks."

Doc Minton's departure left them alone once more. The cell fell silent, neither knowing what to say to the other or if anything needed to be said tonight.

"All right, MacLaren. Time to take off and let this lady have a rest. Come by tomorrow if you

151

want to, but get yourself out of here tonight." Rawlins was bandaged but seemed well enough to bark at everyone.

"All right, Sheriff. I'll check back tomorrow." Jamie stood, gazed down at Victoria for a brief moment, then walked out.

******

"Given the telegram from Delaney, and Hagan's confessions, I doubt the California judge can enforce the warrant. It'll die just as Hagan did. I'll get a message off to San Francisco in the morning. Judge Kinsdale should be back from Phoenix by then. I'm not going to wait for the warrant to be rescinded but I have to clear it with the judge before she can be released." Rawlins said to Sam when the deputy returned a few minutes later.

"Have you told Victoria or Jamie of your decision?"

"Nope. Got to wait until I clear it with Kinsdale tomorrow. But I don't see a problem. It's clear she had nothing to do with Hagan's attempt to murder Wicklin. Maybe Victoria and Jamie can finally work something out." Sheriff Rawlins smiled up at his deputy. Yep, he surely hoped they could.

Chapter Nineteen

"I'd like to speak with Victoria, if she'll let me." Jamie's request was reasonable, but Rawlins just shook his head.

"Can't, Jamie." At the marshal's quizzical expression, Rawlins continued. "Released her this morning. She's at her folks. Guess you'll have to head down that way if you want to speak with her." He wished the boy luck, because he'd need it.

******

Jamie climbed on Rebel for the short distance to the Wright residence, but stopped in front of the Dove. He hesitated only a moment, climbed down and went inside. He needed a drink, maybe two, before confronting Torie and her parents.

At Jamie's look, Ross grabbed a glass, and filled it with whiskey.

Jamie nodded, grabbed the glass, toasted the bartender, and let the golden liquid flow down his throat. What did Niall used call it? Liquid courage? Sounded appropriate to Jamie as he signaled for Ross to pour one more.

"Marshal." Gloria had come up on him without making a sound. Jamie had to admire her. She was the only saloon woman he'd ever met who wore none of the garish makeup so many of them favored. A little rouge. That was it. She was a beautiful woman, and he hoped his friend Sam understood the treasure he was getting.

Sam had confided in him that he and Gloria were talking marriage, but that she was hesitant. She'd planned to sell the saloon and move away. Gloria wanted a fresh start, where no one knew her or her history. Sam didn't want to leave his deputy position, but he'd do whatever was needed to make her happy.

Jamie had listened without saying a word. He understood her concerns but also knew Sam had found a home. Jamie hoped he'd have a chance to speak with Gloria, if not now, then soon. He'd like to convince her to stay in Fire Mountain, with Sam.

"Well, if it isn't the future Mrs. Browning." Jamie smiled and raised his glass to Gloria.

She blushed, which was something you didn't see often. "So he told you, did he?" She rested her hand on the bar and turned to face him. "We're just talking about it you know, may not work out. We'll see."

"He did, and I do believe it will all work out fine."

She smiled while looking around the saloon. "I won't miss this, Jamie," she finally said, "but the life I led here is what will make it possible for us to start fresh, if that's what we decide. Go anywhere we want where no one will know me. I've already started to put the word out. Let me know if you hear of someone interested in a profitable saloon in a good Arizona town." Her smile was so genuine that Jamie found himself wondering if the woman he loved would ever smile at him like that again.

"No problem, Gloria, but, I wish you'd settle here." At her look, he continued. "Look, it's a good town, growing, and Sam has a great job that fits him. People respect him and admire you. Find a place a ways from town where you can do, well, whatever you want to do. You know there are lots of people here who like you. Respect you for what you've achieved."

"But there's just as many who would cheer if I left," she added quietly.

"Those are the same ones who'd cheer if all the saloons closed down. It's not necessarily you, Gloria. They just don't like any of the saloons. But, we have a good number of them and no one's shutting them down anytime soon. Alicia and Kate would be very happy if you stayed, as would a lot of other women."

"Look, Jamie, there's something you should know before you go off thinking Kate would welcome me," Gloria began but Jamie cut her off with a wave of his hand.

"She knows about you and Niall. All of us do. She doesn't hold it against Niall, so why should she hold it against you? Besides, it's in the past. You were there for him when he needed someone. You were his friend, and I know he still sees you as that, even if he can't be a friend to you now." Jamie sipped at his whiskey.

Gloria worked to keep her emotions in check. She hadn't realized all the MacLarens knew of her relationship with Niall. "I never saw him even once while he was married to Camille, and haven't since Kate," she murmured, ashamed of what Jamie may have thought.

His earnest look helped calm her. "We know that, too, Gloria. Like I said, think about it. You have many more friends here than you know." He set the glass down and started for the door.

"Jamie?"

He looked back at her.

"Thanks," Gloria smiled. "And good luck with Victoria. She still loves you, you know." She almost laughed at the surprised look on Jamie's face. "She told me herself, but you better not tell her that."

※※※※※※

"Marshal MacLaren, what can I do for you?" Hen Wright was cordial, but far from the congenial friend Jamie had known his whole life.

"Mr. Wright," Jamie paused, not sure how to proceed, "I, uh, know how you and Mrs. Wright feel about me, and I don't blame you. But I'd like to have a word with Victoria, if she'll see me." The forlorn look on Jamie's face softened Hen, but not enough to excuse all the pain he'd caused Victoria.

"Jamie, I don't know what good it'll do for you to see her. She's finally free. Free of the unfounded charges, humiliation and degradation she's endured the last couple of weeks." Hen hated the way he must sound, but it had to be said. "In our minds, we know it was your job. But, we also believe that a part of you wanted her to be guilty. To suffer a little for all the hurt she caused. But that still doesn't make it right. We thought better of you, Jamie." The sad tone of Hen's voice caused Jamie's stomach to clench. He still wondered at his motivations, and Hen's accusations only emphasized the doubts he had himself.

Jamie swallowed the lump in his throat, and nodded at a man that he respected more than most. But he needed to speak with Torie. He needed to find out if what Gloria had said was true. If she still loved him.

"I understand how you feel about me. I feel that way about myself. Yes, we had a job to do, and yes, a small part of me wanted to see her suffer a little for what she'd done. But that never stopped me from trying to get to the truth. From killing the man who kidnapped her." He stopped, took a deep breath, looked away at the clear night sky, while trying to focus his thoughts. "I love her. I'll always love her. I don't believe she feels the same, but I'll never know if I don't talk to her. Please, just let her know I'm here." It was not quite a plea, but as close to one as Jamie would ever make.

Hen took a long time to respond. His feelings were so mixed. He loved Victoria, but he also cared for the boy standing in front of him. "All right, Jamie. I'll ask, but don't get your hopes up."

He left Jamie standing on the porch while he walked up the stairs to his daughter's room.

"Victoria, Jamie ..." he started to say.

"I know, Papa. He wants to speak with me. I heard what he had to say." Her voice was so soft that Hen had to listen closely to hear her. "I just don't know that I can face him. He'll want answers to things I can't talk about, answers that'll push him further away. Papa, I just don't know that I can do it." Hen wrapped his arm around his daughter, pulling her close.

"It's all right. You don't need to speak with him tonight. Maybe once you've settled in and see that no one feels the less about you, you'll be able to speak with him. He still loves you and deserves an explanation, Victoria. You know he does."

She knew her father spoke the truth. Jamie needed and deserved an explanation. It was only fair that it come from her, but not tonight. "Yes, maybe that's for the best, Papa. Another time." She hugged her father, turned, and went back up the stairs to her room while Hen walked down to deliver the news to Jamie.

"Sorry, Jamie. She's not up to speaking with you tonight. Another time, perhaps."

"I understand. But, you can let her know that I'll keep coming back until she talks to me. I'm not giving up so easily this time."

Chapter Twenty

It was a long, tiring week for Jamie, helping his brothers finish the new barn and a bedroom for baby Adam. He worked each day from dawn to late at night, pounding nails, installing windows and doors, and painting. He stopped to eat, but didn't take many meals with the family. He needed solitude and the grueling pace that this work demanded.

Jamie hadn't tried to see Victoria again. He would soon, but he knew she needed time, and maybe lots of it. From what Sam had said, she took visits from Gloria, and was cordial to Sam. She understood Sam's job had required he arrest her, and she appreciated her treatment while in jail. Beyond that, she offered no indication of what she thought or felt.

"Hey, brother. I'm headed to the Dove for a drink and cards. Join me. Drew's not interested. It's pretty dull going by myself. What do you say?" Will was a good kid. Kid? No, he was a man, and there was no doubt about that. He worked hard and loved the ranch. He'd do anything for his family and had proven it over and over. Jamie owed him some of his time.

"And Emily? How does she feel about you going to the Dove?"

"She's fine with it as long as it's only cards and such. She trusts me, Jamie." Will's smile was broad. He'd asked Emily to marry him and she'd said yes. Jamie was pleased for his brother.

"Sure, Will. Sounds good to me. I need a break and a night in town would do us both good."

An hour later they were walking through the doors of the saloon. The piano player was in the middle of a lively tune, the men were playing cards or just telling each other lies, and laughter was coming from the upstairs rooms. Will was right, it was good to get out for a night.

"Ross," Jamie called out as he and Will walked up to the bar, "give us a bottle and a couple of glasses, if you would."

"Sure enough, Jamie. Good to see you, Will," the bartender grabbed two glasses and the bottle.

"Sam been in?" Jamie asked as he poured the drinks.

"Two to three times a day," Ross chuckled. "Those two are about inseparable. But it's good to see Gloria happy. I hope to hell that deputy ain't planning to break her heart. I'll tell you the truth. If that happens, there's more than one of us who won't take it well." The tone was joking, but the look Ross gave Jamie indicated the man was as serious as they came.

Jamie raised an eyebrow and nodded at the bartender. "I hear what you're saying. I got to say, I've never seen Sam this way. He's crazy about her. If any heart is going to break, it'll be Gloria doing the damage." Jamie turned to Will, who'd been standing wide-eyed at the exchange, toasted his brother, and downed the first of many whiskies.

They had a good time. The brothers played cards, sang along to the piano, and enjoyed the company of the other men as they talked about ranching, politics, and life in a small town. As usual, Will was the life of the party, cracking jokes, teasing the ladies, and laughing more than the rest of them. Neither had accepted invitations to go upstairs. Jamie didn't know if Will had ever ventured in that direction, but at twenty, Jamie guessed he had. Regardless, he doubted his brother's future included any further visits upstairs.

At midnight they said their goodbyes. Their journey required them to ride by the Wright place, and as they neared the house, Jamie noticed a solitary figure sitting on the porch, staring into the night. He recognized Victoria, and pulled Rebel to a stop.

"Will, why don't you ride on to the ranch? I'm going to stop a spell. See if I can visit with Victoria for a minute." Jamie glanced at his brother, who nodded his understanding and turned his horse toward home.

******

Victoria enjoyed this time of night. It was her time alone, when she could think and make decisions about her future. And she loved staring at the stars. Some nights she walked up the hill to the knoll, but tonight she'd decided to sit on the porch and rock.

She turned her gaze away from the sky and he was there. She couldn't face Jamie, not yet. But looking at him, her heart surged and she wanted more than anything to run to him, throw her arms around his neck. She wanted to tell him how much she loved him, missed him, and was so terribly sorry for what had happened years ago. But she couldn't. He was a proud man, always had been. Over the years, she'd convinced herself that he'd reject her once and for all if he knew the whole story.

It was too late to go back into the house. He'd dismounted Rebel. She watched as his long, measured strides brought him closer to the house and up the steps. She'd just have to face him.

"Hello, Victoria," Jamie said as he joined her on the porch. "Mind if I sit a spell?"

She just looked at him as he held his hat in his hands, worried the brim, and waited for her response.

"Please. Have a seat and stay as long as you'd like. I was just going inside." She started to stand but Jamie's words stopped her.

"Don't leave, Torie. Please, stay a bit. We don't have to talk. Just let me be near you for a while."

His words surprised her and tugged at her heart. He seemed so lonely, perhaps as lonely as she felt. She sat back down and pulled a blanket over her legs. It'd been getting colder. Summer was moving to fall with the chillier weather following.

They sat in silence for a long time, both lost in their own thoughts, both too scared to voice what burned in their hearts.

"I'm so sorry, Jamie." Victoria spoke first, saying the only thing she could.

"Me too, Torie," Jamie reached over to take her hand in his. He squeezed lightly, but didn't let go. He never wanted to let go.

It was several minutes before Jamie spoke again.

"I went crazy when you married Wicklin. Did things I'm ashamed of, but I finally realized that you just never loved me, and needed something else. Things I couldn't give you and would never be able to give you."

"That's not true, Jamie," Torie protested softly. "I did love you. Loved you more than you could ever understand. But I had no choice." Her voice was filled with remorse.

"You had choices, Torie, Wicklin or me, and you chose him." He clasped her hand tighter, afraid this might be the last time he'd ever get to touch her. She was free to leave for California, if that's what she decided. He still loved her, but had no hold on her. "You should know I found out about the plans your parents and his aunt had for you to wed Wicklin. That's why I never came after you. It became clear to me that I never had a chance." His voice was calm but full of regret.

It surprised her that he'd learned that much. Few people knew of the letters or the real reason behind Hamilton coming to Fire Mountain. "I never knew about the arrangement, Jamie, and Mama and Papa never agreed to it. They wrote his aunt, but never approved of a marriage. He came anyway, at his aunt's urging." She fingered the cloth in her pocket. It'd been her constant companion for years, her only connection to Jamie. It was threadbare, but still she clung to it, refusing to break her ties to the past. "When I told them I'd decided to marry Hamilton, my parents tried to talk me out of it. But it was too late. I couldn't change what had happened."

"What happened, Torie? Tell me what happened to make you decide for Wicklin and not me."

The tears came unbidden even as she sought to control her raging emotions.

"Oh, Jamie, I wish I was stronger, more like you. But I'm not. I'm weak, just as I was that night. I can't undo any of it. If I could, I would." She pulled loose of Jamie's grip and buried her head in her hands, sobbing uncontrollably.

Jamie stood and lifted her into his arms. Sitting back down he settled her on his lap, while she continued to sob. She wrapped her arms around his neck and buried her head in his shoulder.

"It's all right, honey." Jamie tried to sooth her, rubbing her back with slow circles and keeping her close. Although she still hadn't provided a reason for her change of heart, he now felt certain there was more to it than he'd always thought. Maybe it was the money, but perhaps it wasn't. He'd give

164

her time, let her tell him when she felt ready. It'd been seven years since he had lost her. He could wait a little longer if it meant getting her back.

Her body relaxed as the crying slowed. She lay very still in his arms, her breathing steady as she continued to clutch at his shirt. He never wanted to let her go.

"I do love you, Jamie. I've always loved you." Her words were muffled against his chest.

Jamie placed a kiss on her hair, then her forehead, and moved to her temple before caressing her cheek with his lips. She lifted her face to his and his mouth closed over hers. It was a soft caress at first, but became more demanding as she parted her lips to give him access.

He deepened the kiss and their tongues tangled, causing her to burrow closer to him. Her arms wrapped possessively around his neck, and both moaned at the intimacy they were creating. He pulled her closer as one hand moved to her stomach, then up to cup the underside of her breast through the fabric of her dress. He stroked it gently before moving to cup the other one. A deep sigh escaped her lips as he continued to caress her.

Jamie came to his senses first and pulled back, taking a deep breath, while settling her back against his shoulder.

"Torie, sweetheart, I want you as much as always. But, if we keep on like this, I'm going to take you right here on your parents' porch, and I don't want our first time to be that way. When we make love, and we will make love, it's going to be right. And, it's going to be soon." He paused to place another kiss in her hair. "Make no mistake. I'm not letting you go this time."

If only that could be true, Victoria thought, as she took a deep breath and closed her eyes.

******

Morning came early for Jamie, but he hadn't felt this good about life in a long time. After Victoria fell asleep in his arms, he sat on the porch for a long time, not willing to let her go. An hour passed before he stood, opened the front door, and carried her into the house. He laid her on the sofa and covered her with a blanket before placing another kiss on her forehead. He wished he could take her up to her room, but he'd already gone as far as he dared. She was sound asleep when he left.

There was still much she hadn't told him. He knew that whatever the secret, her fear of telling him seemed worse than her fear of losing him. That had to change. They could never have a future if she didn't reveal the truth of the past. She said she loved him, had always loved him. He couldn't shake the feeling that she'd spoken the truth.

Today he'd help his brothers finish painting, cleanup, then head into town to see if she'd allow him to escort her to supper. He knew he may be rushing her, and if she just wanted to sit outside for a while, that was fine too. Whatever she wanted was fine with him.

Chapter Twenty-One

"What do you mean, she's gone?" Jamie was stunned at Hen's words. Victoria had left. Packed her things and taken the morning stage. She had refused to confide in her parents, just said she had to leave. There were things that needed tending to, she'd told them.

"Did she leave any word for me?" The pain started, deep in his chest. His stomach clenched, and all he could think was that he'd lost her again.

"No, she didn't. I'm sorry, Jamie." Hen scrubbed a hand over his tired face. It was obvious he was as upset about her leaving as Jamie.

"I see." Jamie plunged his hands into his pockets and walked back to Rebel. He couldn't come to grips with her leaving him, again. The pain turned to anger, then to resolve. She couldn't run again. This time he knew with certainty that he wouldn't let her go so easily. He'd leave for San Francisco today.

******

Victoria sat in the train's passenger car on her way north to San Francisco, and again berated herself for being such a coward. This time she was running because she was scared that once Jamie learned the truth, he'd walk away from her as she'd once walked away from him. Had she made another mistake, leaving Fire Mountain and a possible future with him?

Aunt Bea had always said she'd turned out to be a very strong woman. She'd tolerated Hamilton's abuse, but still held her head high, and had found a place in the hearts of their friends. They'd embraced her, even while shunning her husband.

She already knew what her life would be like with Jamie. He was the man she'd always wanted— strong, capable, smart, and devoted—everything she'd ever desired, and he was offering himself to her, at a price. Tell him the truth about why she'd married Hamilton. What if she did tell Jamie the truth, and he rejected her, walked away? Would she be any worse off than she was now? No, she decided, she wouldn't.

Victoria ticked off what needed to be done when she arrived in San Francisco the following day. First, she'd work with Mr. Dunsford to file divorce papers and get the estate in order so that she could handle it from Arizona. She'd find someone to help her sell the restaurant, close the house, and find positions for the remaining staff. All were within her power and she was certain Mr. Dunsford would support her on these decisions. Then she'd run home to Jamie and pray that he'd take her back this time.

******

He sat near the rear of the train, in the furthest passenger area available, able to check on her a couple of cars up. She never looked back or suspected he was there, with her, protecting her. She slept in her seat, as did he, but took her meals in the dining car. He was careful to stagger the meals so she never saw him. But he watched everything she did, and knew he'd made the right decision.

"Next stop, San Francisco, main station," the conductor called as he made his way through the cars. Jamie sat ready. As soon as she got off, he'd already be on the walkway, waiting to follow her. He needed to know what she planned to do. Surely she wouldn't go back to Wicklin. No, she wanted away from him, Jamie was certain of it. She had other plans. He just needed to discover what they were.

"Hello, Mrs. Wicklin. It's so good to see you again and know that you're safe. Are you well?" It was an older gentleman reaching out to take her bags and escort her to a waiting buggy. Damn, why hadn't Jamie thought that she'd have someone waiting for her? He needed to find transportation, but where?

"Would you be MacLaren? Jamie MacLaren?" The voice came from behind him. He turned to see a medium sized man with thinning, light colored hair walk up and extend his hand.

"Jefferson Delaney. You may not remember me. Sam Browning wired that you'd be coming in and asked that I watch for you."

Jamie clasped the man's hand, glad to know that Sam had contacted the ex-Pinkerton agent.

"Delaney, good to see you again. It's been a long time." Jamie looked behind him in the direction Victoria had headed.

"Don't worry. The man is Silas Dunsford, the attorney, and I bet I know just where they're going. Come on, we'll follow far enough behind so they don't see us, but close enough to make sure of their destination." Delaney grabbed Jamie's bag and headed to a waiting carriage.

******

Thirty minutes later they watched as Victoria and Dunsford disappeared into a stately building in the central business district.

"Dunsford's office is on the third floor, looks out onto the street. They released him from the hospital a week ago and the man has scarcely left his office since. I'm guessing he's trying to reconstruct the aunt's file, but I can't get in to see him. The assistant has him locked up tighter than if he were in jail." Delaney continued forward and motioned for Jamie to follow.

Not long after, they were seated in an empty office next door to Dunsford's, listening through an old opening that had once connected the two offices.

"He's been working alone most of the time, so nothing to hear except the rustling of papers." Delaney's voice was barely above a whisper. "But today, with Mrs. Wicklin joining him, perhaps we'll hear something useful. Not that we need anything more as she's been cleared of the charges. Nonetheless, maybe you need to learn more to move on, if you get my meaning." It was said in such a casual tone that Jamie almost missed the implication. This was about helping Jamie make a decision, nothing more.

Jamie looked at Delaney, nodded his understanding, and thanked Sam again for connecting with his old friend.

"Victoria, your idea to keep a copy of Beatrice's will at the bank was brilliant. Wicklin had no idea of its existence. We must work with one of the few bankers that isn't in his pocket." Dunsford sounded simultaneously pleased and disgusted. "I don't know how so many people were taken in by your husband. They all must have speculated he was the sole beneficiary of the estate. Just plain greed, that's what I believe."

Jamie and Jefferson looked at each other upon hearing that a copy of the will had been hidden from Wicklin. And it had been done at Victoria's suggestion.

"Regardless, here it is and the time has come to share its contents with you." Dunsford said. Jamie and Jefferson could hear the rustling of papers through the small opening.

"Wait, Silas. First, please tell me how you're doing. Are you well, and recovered?" Victoria had always held great affection for this man. He'd done his best to educate her on handling financial matters. On numerous occasions he'd placed himself in danger by acting as a buffer between Victoria and her husband.

"I'm doing quite well, Victoria. Once I regained consciousness, I healed quickly and was released within a week. In the end, this was perhaps the best solution for everyone. Wicklin's in jail, you're free to live your life in San Francisco in the style you deserve, and I'm free of an obnoxious, disreputable individual. All is as it should be." He smiled as he sat down and began his review.

In the next room Jamie grimaced at the revelation that Victoria planned to stay in California, permanently severing her ties with him.

"Beatrice was a very practical woman. She worked hard, expecting others to do the same. However, she was also a forgiving soul and understood that not all people were meant to achieve to the same level. The provisions of the will provided for many people. Those bequeaths were made upon her death. The bulk of the estate was set up so that if you stayed married to her nephew for seven years, you'd receive everything that remained, and it's substantial." He adjusted the wire-rimmed glasses. "No additional provisions were made for Hamilton. It's completely up to you how you proceed with the estate. Beatrice was quite firm on that language."

Victoria sat quietly with her hands folded in her lap. She didn't know what to make of it. Her acquaintance with Aunt Bea had lasted a few short years, yet she'd left her so much. Why? "I don't understand why she would leave it all to me."

"She had great respect and empathy for you, Victoria, and she was deeply ashamed of what had happened as a result of her reckless demand that Hamilton marry a woman of quality. She also regretted her communications with your parents that ended with Hamilton traveling to Arizona. I won't go into specifics, as we both know the trials you endured, but you need to know that she wasn't oblivious to your situation. She regretted all of it most ardently in the last months of her life. I believe those were the main reasons for the directions in her will." Dunsford stopped to take a drink of water.

"I see," she said in a voice just above a whisper. Her mind raced at the implications of Aunt Bea's decisions.

"This is an accounting of her estate." He handed her a set of documents. "It is quite current. I'm sure you'll need some time to review all the details, but let me say that you're quite a wealthy woman, Victoria."

Jamie sat stone still in the next room. He felt as if all the air had been sucked out of the small space he occupied. He couldn't get a breath, couldn't comprehend the extent of what he'd heard. She was now a wealthy, independent woman who was accepted into the highest social circles of the city. Now that she was free of Hamilton, there'd be no reason for her to return to Arizona or him.

The contents of these documents were a complete surprise to Victoria. She was staggered at the provisions Aunt Bea had made for her. Everything went to her, to do with as she pleased. She could sell everything and move wherever she wanted, or continue to live in the city. Aunt Bea had simply wanted her to have the freedom of choice, something she'd lost when she married Hamilton.

"So it's true then." She stared at the papers Silas had handed her. "What I was told is true. After seven years, if I remained married to Hamilton, it all came to me."

"It's true, Victoria."

"But what if I hadn't stayed with him, or if something had happened to me? If I had gone to jail, or died?"

"Oh, that was quite simple. In the event anything happened other than you staying married to him for the full seven years, the entire estate was to be divided between her favorite charities. The woman was quite thorough. By the time the will was finalized, she had made up her mind that Hamilton should get nothing. Ever." Silas smiled as he recalled the endless meetings his client had requested to be sure everything was just as she desired.

"Why am I learning of this now? Why not earlier?"

"Unfortunately, the provisions of the will stated that you not to be told until the seven years had elapsed, and then only if you were still married to Wicklin. I cannot give you a good explanation of her decision on the matter or why the seven years.

174

But now you're under no further obligation to that miserable piece of humanity."

Dunsford paused as if trying to decide how to phrase his next words. "But what's always been a curiosity to me, Victoria, is why you stayed with him. He couldn't have been easy to live with."

There was complete silence, leaving Jamie to wonder if she planned to answer.

"It's really quite simple, Silas. Hamilton threatened to kill my parents and Jamie MacLaren if I ever left him. It was the same threat he'd made when he forced me to marry him. He had contacts and wealth. I knew he could do as he threatened. They are the three most important people in my life. I couldn't take a chance he'd do as he said. He made sure I understood he always knew what they were doing. His connections seemed endless. It was his way of keeping me in my place, by letting me know he could get to any of them whenever he chose. It may have been the only positive thing to come out of the marriage. I learned that my parents were doing well, and that Jamie had become some type of hired gun before joining the U.S. Marshal Service. It was hard to learn he'd moved on, without me. But, what else could he do? At least he's alive." She twisted the small cloth she clutched in her hands and looked up at Dunsford. "So you see? What other choice did I have?"

Jamie's fists clenched as he listened from the other room. She had left him to save his life. To save his damned life, and it had almost killed him anyway. He was both relieved and furious with her for not trusting his ability to take care of her and himself. He needed time to decide how he felt about the two of them and their future now that the truth was out.

"Mrs. Wicklin is quite a wealthy woman, MacLaren, and innocent of the knowledge about the seven years. Her statements to you and Sam seem to have been proven true." Delaney said as they continued to sit in the second office.

Yes, Victoria was a very wealthy woman and he was a U.S. Marshal. It was a good living, but he'd never be able to provide for her in the style her new wealth allowed. Even the ranch, which did well and was expected to grow substantially, had to support all the MacLarens plus all of the hands. If he left the Marshals Service as he'd planned, he'd be added to the list of people the ranch supported. And if he married...No, that wasn't a remote possibility now. Not with what he knew of Victoria's new financial position.

"You okay, MacLaren?" Delaney whispered in his ear.

"Yea, I've heard enough. Let's go," Jamie said through clenched teeth. He needed air, a drink, and time to think through everything he'd learned. He had come to San Francisco to fetch Torie home, but now he understood that he might be making the trip back alone.

******

Victoria was exhausted. She'd been with Silas until late in the night, discussing her plans to sell the business properties, close the house, and move back to Fire Mountain. He understood and helped her map out a strategy so that he could take care of selling the business while she concentrated on her move. Dunsford estimated it would take no more than four to six weeks, then she could leave. It wasn't as soon as she desired, but at least everything had started to move in the direction she wanted.

Dunsford expressed concern she wasn't giving herself enough time to enjoy her new freedom, to see if a life in the city might make her happy, but she'd been firm. She'd never been more sure of a decision in her life. The man she loved was in Arizona, and she was running back to him as fast as she could.

All but one of the few servants she'd employed had left, not knowing the outcome of her fate, but Dunsford had notified her personal maid, Penelope, of her return. At least the house was clean, there was food available, and her bed had been turned down with her nightclothes set out. Penelope had always been efficient.

She walked into her room and closed the door. Her eyes moved slowly around the room, settling on the glow from the fireplace. Victoria set her small satchel down and walked toward the flames. It was over, truly over, and now she was free to make her own choices. Free to build her own life. And the life she wanted was with Jamie.

******

177

He'd had several drinks more than he intended before taking a carriage to the address Delaney had provided. Jamie asked the driver twice if he was certain the house in front of him belonged to Mr. and Mrs. Wicklin. The driver confirmed the address and Jamie got down, not quite sure why he'd come.

She lived in a mansion. It spanned a full city block with gardens all around and fountains on two sides. There were at least two stories and balconies all around. He walked, unseen, through the property, wincing with each new revelation of Torie's wealth. The lights were on downstairs and he could see a light in one of the upstairs rooms.

At the sound of horses, Jamie walked to the corner of the house and peered around. Torie. She'd just descended from the carriage. A door opened and a slight, young maid appeared to take her mistress's belongings, gushing at how much Victoria had been missed. Servants. Jamie hadn't even thought of the servants she'd have to leave behind if he took her back home. The door closed. He watched as several lights downstairs went dark and more lights on the second floor were lit.

He sat on a garden bench, his head in his hands, staring down at his dirty boots and work pants. He hadn't even taken the time to change before following her. His heart felt heavy. Jamie knew there'd never be another love for him like Victoria. The seven years without her had already proven it to him. Looking up, he stared at a house he could never expect to own. A lifestyle he couldn't provide. Resigned, he stood and walked out the gate to the street.

He'd leave tomorrow without her ever knowing he'd come. It would be better this way. Better for both of them.

Chapter Twenty-Two

Weeks had passed since Jamie had returned home. The trip hadn't gone as he'd anticipated. The disappointment at not bringing Victoria home with him had worked on his heart much more harshly than expected. Perhaps because now he knew she was available to marry again, just not to him.

Hen notified him that since Wicklin and Victoria had been married in Arizona, Jerrod Minton was handling her divorce. Jerrod saw no reason it wouldn't be granted, but he'd heard nothing of her returning to Fire Mountain. Neither had Hen nor Anna. Jamie resigned himself to accept her decision.

Jamie needed to move on. He'd tendered his resignation, gotten drunk several nights in a row, sat up until dawn talking lies to Sam, Will or Niall, or whomever would listen, and was now back to being a part-owner of the largest spread in northern Arizona.

Maybe his older brother was right. The weeks since coming home had given him time to think about marrying someone else, raising a family, and doing his best to find what Niall and Kate had found. He decided he wanted that life, wanted children. Jamie was ready to finally cut the ties from his past and start fresh.

******

"Where you off to, Jamie, all gussied up and smelling good?" Will nearly fell over himself at the sight of his older brother. It was Saturday night, but he didn't look like he'd be heading to any saloon.

"Oh, he didn't tell you, Will?" Alicia walked in from the kitchen drying her hands on a soft cotton towel. "He's having dinner in town with some woman he met. Can't believe he didn't mention it to you." Alicia winked at Niall and Kate who were sitting together playing with Adam, trying to suppress their laughter. It was good to see Jamie get out, get on with his life.

"He surely did not. Who is she, Jamie? Do I know her?" Will was still sizing him up.

"Will, you know just about every pretty female between ten and forty in this town, so I'd guess you know this one," Niall teased as he picked up Adam, laying the baby carefully over his shoulder to burp him.

"Hey, I'm getting married. I don't look at all the pretty women any more. Don't be spreading lies about me, big brother." Will laughed along with his family. He'd never felt so good and it appeared the rest of the family felt the same.

Jamie just smiled at the scene. Yes, he'd made the right choice, coming home to be with his family. And he was looking forward to tonight. She was a pretty thing, and new to town. He'd been lucky to spot her as she emerged from the stage.

Took him all week to talk her into letting him escort her to dinner. He actually felt nervous.

"Well, I'm heading out," he said to the others as he donned his best hat to leave for town.

"Hey, you didn't tell me who she is," Will yelled after him. "I'm going to see Emily. We could go with you to dinner, meet the woman."

"Another time, Will. Tonight it's just me and the lady." Jamie mounted Rebel and started for town.

******

Jamie and the very pretty woman sat across from each other in the dining room at Hen's hotel. He'd been trying to figure out the color of her hair. It seemed the color of a deep red sky at sunset with streaks of sunlight. Her dark green eyes reminded him of the local pines, and her porcelain skin glowed in the candlelight. He guessed she was about five- foot-seven inches, just the right size for his six-foot-one frame. She was a teacher and had just taken the local position after the last teacher had married a rancher down near Phoenix.

"So, Madeleine, how do you like it here so far?" Jamie asked as he looked at her over the rim of his coffee cup. They'd finished dinner and were working on the last bites of dessert.

"I've not had much opportunity to see the sights but I'm sure I'll like it just fine." Her green eyes focused on his as she spoke. She knew full well that he was interested in her even if she'd only met him a few days ago. Madeleine had learned he was an ex-marshal from a much respected ranching family. They were well off, but not wealthy. He was one of the most gorgeous men she'd ever met. His rugged good looks complemented his strong, muscled body. He wouldn't have any trouble attracting women, just like her ex-fiancé hadn't. She was interested in getting to know Jamie MacLaren better, but her heart told her to take it slow. No sense making the same mistake she'd made before. It'd been two years, but the pain still reminded her to be cautious.

"Well, we can change that quick enough. If you have no other plans, I'd like to bring the buggy into town next Saturday and take you around the country, show you the sights, maybe head over to the ranch. How does that sound?"

"That would be lovely, Jamie," she said, mentally reminding herself that she was going to take this one day at time.

******

"No, Silas. I'm not staying another two weeks. I'll be on the train tomorrow. I won't change my plans one more time. The papers can be sent to me in Fire Mountain. I'll work with Jerrod to finish it all up and send everything back to you." Victoria had planned to leave over a week ago, but delays had interrupted her trip. Now she was determined to leave no matter what Silas said.

"Fine, Victoria, if you're sure that's what you still want to do. But I don't see how a few more days could impact your plans with Mr. MacLaren. Believe me, the man will never be able to find a woman to replace you, no matter where he looks, and certainly not in a small town in the territory. He'll be there, still single, and waiting for you." Silas had grown quite fond of Victoria through their years of working together. He'd miss her, but understood her desire to go home and be with the man she'd always loved.

"I wish I had the same confidence, Silas. You haven't met Jamie. Believe me, he's someone any single woman would want. Mama told me he's resigned his position to become a part of the family ranch. Now all the available women are trying to attract his attention. I don't plan to let anyone else have him, Silas. Not as long as there is a single breath left in me." She smiled at one of the best men she'd ever had the privilege to meet and hoped their paths would cross many more times in the future.

******

"Another date with the lovely Madeleine so soon, Jamie? You do move fast when you put your mind to it." Niall slapped him on the back as he walked past to saddle Zeus.

"Just a buggy ride to show her the sites. She hasn't had time to see much, and as far as I know, doesn't own a buggy or horse. I'll be back by mid-afternoon if you need help with anything." Jamie climbed up into the buggy and snapped the reins lightly.

It turned out to be one of those beautiful fall days without the cold wind of winter. They'd have some snow off and on for a few months, then the weather would turn warm again as the mountains changed to the bright green of spring. That was Torie's favorite time of year. His heart still ached a little when he thought of her or someone mentioned her name. Jamie needed to put every trace of her firmly in his past.

He was glad he'd made the decision to go on with his life. No doubt she'd already forgotten him in favor of one of the rich available gentlemen in her social circle. At least she no longer haunted his every thought, keeping him awake at night and messing with his mind during the day.

The sunrise didn't remind him of her golden hair quite as often, or the way he'd always loved running his hands through the long, silky strands. Aunt Alicia's Sunday dress with shades of violet didn't induce images of Torie's beautiful eyes, or how they lit up whenever anyone told a lie or made her laugh. She'd always been a fireball when you got her going, and he used to love teasing her when they were young. But they weren't young any more, he reminded himself. And she didn't seem to be the fireball he remembered. Stronger, more determined, still as beautiful, but the spontaneous, carefree girl of his past was gone. She was a woman now, settled in her opulent mansion in the city, enjoying a life far removed from his.

******

By the time he reached Madeleine's cottage behind the schoolhouse, the day no longer looked so beautiful and his enthusiasm for the ride had subsided quite a bit. At this moment he just wanted to show her around for a couple of hours before heading home. Jamie didn't want to analyze it too much but something had changed.

He jumped down from the buggy as Madeleine came out the front door carrying a basket.

"Morning, Madeleine. You look lovely today."

And she did. She wore a green dress that matched her eyes, with long sleeves and lace cuffs. The lacy bodice showed just enough to let him know that God had not skimped in that area. Her hair was pinned up with a silver clip and a few strands of curls flowed down her back in soft cascades of several shades of red. He wanted to take the clip out and run his hands through it to see if it felt as soft as Torie's. Jamie stopped his train of thought to focus back on the women in front of him. She carried a parasol and shawl, and also had a large blanket slung over her arm. The lady came prepared.

"Good morning, Jamie. It's a beautiful day. Thank you so much for offering me a tour. I brought a picnic, if that's all right." She smiled up at him. It was a beautiful smile filled with warmth, but it wasn't the face he expected.

"Jamie? Is everything all right?" Madeleine asked as he stood staring at her.

"Uh, yes, everything's just fine. A picnic sounds good. Let me help you up and we'll be on our way." Jamie shook off, once again, his thoughts of Torie, and forced himself to concentrate on the woman in front of him. He liked her and wanted to get to know her. She could be just the woman for him. He needed to give her a chance, give himself a chance, but he realized this transition would take more time than he'd thought.

"Jamie, would you mind if we stopped at the mercantile for a couple of things? Won't take long."

"Of course." He guided the buggy to the mercantile located next to the hotel. Jamie helped Madeleine down, and escorted her inside. She started down one of the aisles as Jamie continued to the counter. He spotted Hen instantly. Although he and Anna owned both the mercantile and hotel, it was seldom you saw either at the small store.

"Morning, Mr. Wright. I'm surprised to see you here and not at the hotel. How are you doing?" Jamie held out his hand, hoping his old friend would not refuse it.

Hen took Jamie's hand in a warm grip. "Real fine, Jamie. Real fine, indeed. Needed to check some things here at the store and Walt wanted some time off, so here I am. Had a surprise passenger on the stage late yesterday. Just got in and was about to head out to..." that's all Hen got out when Victoria walked out from the back. She stopped mid-stride, eyes coming to rest on Jamie's, all the wind rushing out of her lungs. She took a deep breath to steady herself.

He was in shock. She was here, right in front of him and he couldn't move a muscle if he tried. It was worse than being confronted by a drunk with a loaded gun. That he knew he could handle. He wasn't as sure about this. His heart was racing so fast he thought it would jump out of his chest.

"Hello, Jamie." Victoria hesitated before slowly walking towards him. "I was just getting ready to come see you at the ranch..." then her eyes took in a beautiful woman with striking red hair.

"Jamie, would you like peach or berry preserves with your biscuits?" Madeleine called out as she started toward them, holding two tins while looking at the labels. She stopped and looked first at Jamie, then the woman in front of him.

"Jamie," she wound her arm through his and looked up at her escort, "are you going to introduce us?"

"Uh, yes. Madeleine, this is Victoria Wright, I mean Wicklin. Victoria, this is Madeleine Rutherford. She's our new school teacher."

Torie smiled at Madeleine, but it didn't quite reach her eyes. "I'm Hen and Anna Wright's daughter. They own this mercantile as well as the hotel. Jamie and I grew up together, but we haven't seen much of each other for quite a while. I've been visiting in San Francisco. Just returned home last night."

Visiting? Just returned? Home? The words played over in Jamie's head. She sounded as if she'd planned to return all along. Had he been wrong about the reason for her leaving?

"Miss Rutherford?" Hen interjected. "Is that all you'll be needing today?"

Madeleine tore her eyes from Victoria long enough to place the tins on the counter.

"How much?" Jamie tried to focus his thoughts as he fished in his pocket for coins and counted out what Hen requested.

"Well, it was a pleasure, Mrs. Wicklin. I'm sure I'll be seeing you around town." Madeleine took the package Hen offered and turned her gaze up to Jamie.

In an instant, Madeleine's gracious smile and adoring look at Jamie changed all of Victoria's plans. He'd moved on. No longer wanted her. She'd waited too long to come home.

Jamie finally found his voice. "Victoria, how long will you be in town this trip? Will we have some time to visit or is your calendar already full?"

Victoria looked at Madeleine, then back to Jamie, ignoring his question. "Enjoy your picnic, Jamie. It's a lovely day and you have a beautiful woman with you. We'll catch up another time." She turned and walked to the back room, closing the door softly behind her.

Chapter Twenty-Three

Jamie dropped Madeleine off at her cottage around three that afternoon. He begged off coming inside for coffee. His mind had been consumed with the need to see if Torie would speak with him. He couldn't have mistaken the pain he saw in her eyes when she looked at him with Madeleine. The letdown she tried to conceal was all too apparent to him. He knew her too well. What could she be thinking after seeing him with Madeleine?

Madeleine had him laughing a great deal during their time together. She kept the conversation going but wasn't chatty, just fun to be around. Beautiful, and from what he could tell, generous and smart. Any man would want to be with her. Any man except Jamie.

He drove the buggy to the Wright's home, but Hen told him she'd taken a room at the hotel. Her parents were disappointed, but she'd said she needed time to think, decide what to do next. Hen implied that her seeing Jamie with Madeleine had changed Victoria's plans.

"It was just a buggy ride. She's the new teacher and she doesn't have any transportation. How was I to know that Torie would show up? She left without a word and has been gone for weeks. Hell, what a mess." He ran his hand through his hair in a gesture of pure frustration.

"I understand, son. Best you go find her and explain. Something tells me she came back just for you."

Jamie went straight to the hotel, asking for Mrs. Wicklin, but was told she'd gone out. Would he like to leave a message? No, Jamie had replied, he'd come back.

As he turned to leave he noticed one of the hotel clerks, stopped him, and whispered briefly in his ear. The young man nodded, and cast Jamie a quick smile before dashing up the stairs to the upper rooms.

Jamie settled himself in the hotel dining room and waited for an answer to his request. He didn't wait long.

"She's in room two-two-five, Mr. MacLaren, but she's out right now. One of the other employees told me she went to dinner with Sam Browning and his fiancée."

"Thanks for letting me know which room. Is the rest all taken care of?" Jamie had given the boy explicit instructions. The clerk's smile was wide.

"Of course, Mr. MacLaren Here's the key. But if the manager finds out, I'll lose my job." The young man sounded anxious.

"He'll never hear it from me. Thanks for your help." He handed the boy a gold coin as he stood, and headed straight up the stairs to room two-two-five.

******

Victoria inserted the key to her room in the lock about ten o'clock. She was tired but glad Gloria had asked her to join her and Sam for dinner. Facing her parents this evening after the encounter with Jamie was more than she could endure. They'd want to know if seeing him with someone else had changed her plans to stay. Honestly, she just didn't know, but dinner with Gloria and Sam had helped her sort out her thoughts.

"You love him, you know. You always have. And Jamie feels the same. He's never wavered all these years. Believe me, taking a woman on a picnic won't change the man's heart." Gloria stopped at the look from Sam. "Ok, dinner at the hotel and a picnic. Still, not anything that would change the way you two feel. You're back. He's turned in his badge to help with the ranch. It's time, Victoria. Find him. Tell him the truth." Gloria smiled and hugged her friend.

"She's right, Victoria. Jamie's not one to change his feelings in a few weeks. Give it time. I'm sure it'll work out for you two the way it worked out for us." Sam smiled at Gloria and put his arm around her. Victoria was so happy for both of them. They'd made the decision to marry and stay so that Sam could continue in his job. It was the best news Victoria had heard since her return.

She'd made the right decision to stay at the hotel. After seeing Jamie with the other woman, she needed time to think and decide how to approach him and what to say. Gloria and Sam were probably right about Jamie's feelings, but what if they weren't? It had taken her six weeks to handle the property and finances. What if he'd finally grown tired of waiting and found someone else?

She closed the door, noticing that candlelight flickered from the table by the bed. The fireplace glowed and a soft scent of roses floated through the air.

The candles and fire cast just enough light to see, so she took off her wrap while walking toward the fireplace to warm her hands. It wasn't cold outside, but still she felt a chill.

"You know I ought to throttle you for running away again, Torie."

She jumped at the sound of the familiar voice, deep and sensual. Her heart raced as she turned to look towards a dark corner where a figure was barely visible.

"I tell you how I feel, and what do you do? You bolt. Take off for San Francisco." His voice was like steel, unforgiving. He stood and stalked toward her, his grey eyes intent, taking his time.

"Jamie, I can explain..." she started but he silenced her with an angry glare.

"Don't make any more excuses, Torie. I know about Wicklin's threats to have me killed." At her shocked look he continued. "I neither want nor need your protection. Never did. And you damn well knew it seven years ago. What I do need is the real reason you married Wicklin."

When she hesitated, he grabbed her arms and pulled her within a few inches of him.

"Now, Torie. No more waiting. I want to hear it from you." His unsmiling face told her there would be no more chances.

This is it then, she thought. *I'll tell him and he'll walk.* But he was right. He needed to know, deserved to know.

Without preamble, she told him the simple truth. "He raped me, Jamie. Raped me and said he'd tell you that I had offered myself to him." She paused, remembering that night and Hamilton's words. "He said if I didn't marry him he'd kill you and my parents." She stood erect and looked him the eyes as the story unfolded. Tears glistened but she fought to keep her emotions controlled, closed. At least when he left the last thing he'd see would be her standing tall, no longer a scared victim.

The truth slammed into Jamie. He'd suspected it, but always pushed it out of his mind. It had been easier to believe she'd left him for the bastard's money. Her leaving because she wanted Hamilton was one thing, but her leaving because another man forced himself on her was something different. It meant he'd not been able to protect her, save her from the actions of a depraved man. It had always been too painful to face that possibility. But now he had to face it. It made him want to murder Hamilton Wicklin himself, saving San Francisco the trouble of dealing with such a sorry piece of human flesh.

Jamie released her and stepped back. They'd planned to marry. He should've taken care of her, protected her, but he'd failed. Failed miserably, and Torie had paid a horrible price. Now he needed to convince her that he still wanted her, loved her more than life. But her defensive stance told him she had prepared herself for his rejection.

Victoria watched as his expression changed from one of surprise, to anger, then hurt, and finally acceptance. She held her breath and waited for his response.

Jamie's features softened as he walked forward a step and wrapped his fingers in hers. He stood looking at her, his thumbs rubbing circles on the back of each hand, sending electricity up her arms. Then he pulled her to him, wrapped his arms around her, and buried his face in her hair.

"Ah, Torie. Did you think I wouldn't want you after what Wicklin did? That I'd no longer love you? You must've thought my love for you very weak." He stroked her back and placed soft kisses in her hair, breathing in her unique scent. "Even then, when it happened, I would've stood by you, married you. I loved you. I can only think that I failed by not giving you a reason to wait for me to come back." She started to pull away, but he held her to him. "You must have believed I would walk away, be too angry, and believe his lies. If you'd trusted me, you would've had faith in me. I'm sorry, Torie. I failed you in the most basic way."

He did let her go this time when she edged back and looked into his eyes as tears streamed down her cheeks. "You were such a proud man, Jamie. We'd waited to make love until our wedding night. I thought you'd despise me for coming to you ruined. Many men would. I'm sorry. So sorry I didn't trust you. I know now that your reaction couldn't have been worse than the pain I felt in leaving you. All the years without you."

"It's going to be all right now. We're older, but we have the same love as before. We'll work this out, sweetheart." His hands stroked her arms, rested on her shoulders and pulled her to him. His lips brushed across hers, once, twice, then settled more firmly to sip at her bottom lip, sucking it in. His hands had come up to cup either side of her head, holding her still so he could take what he wanted. She opened for him. His tongue swept into her mouth, moving in and out until she caught it and sucked it in with greedy passion.

"God, Torie. I want, need to make love to you. Will you let me?"

She didn't hesitate. "Make love to me Jamie. We'll start our life right now. No more waiting," she breathed against his mouth as she wrapped her arms around his neck and drew him down to her in an invitation that had taken so long to offer.

He scooped her into his arms and carried her to the bed, setting her down and turning her away from him. "I want to undress you," he whispered into her ear as he placed feathery kisses down her neck. He made short work of the buttons, kissing his way down her back to just above her pantalets, pushing the dress over her hips and down her legs until it lay in a heap on the floor. His hands returned to release the fastenings of her camisole. It followed her dress to the floor. Strong arms wrapped around her, pulling her flush to his chest while his hands cupped her breasts, teasing and caressing.

She turned in his arms and captured his head to pull him down for a long, drugging kiss. His hands moved up her arms, pushing her far enough away so his gaze could wander from the long curve of her neck, to the full globes of her breasts, and down to her trim waist and rounded hips.

"Ah, Torie, you are so beautiful. More beautiful than I could've ever imagined." He began to pull her back towards him before Torie stopped him.

"You still have all your clothes on. I want to see you, too. Touch you."

Jamie smiled, then gently moved her backwards so that she could sit on the edge of the bed. He pulled his shirt from his pants and began to work the buttons.

"Wait, let me." Torie stood, her hands reaching for his shirt, her fingers working the buttons, releasing them one at a time until she could spread the fabric wide and place her palms on his warm chest. She stroked in small circles, learning the feel of him, creating a path of heat that followed her hands around his chest to his back as she pulled him to her. His course chest hair felt wonderful against her skin. She pulled away, moving her hands so she could use the pads of her fingers to explore his nipples, causing him to curse softly before grabbing her hands in his and pinning them to her sides.

"Enough. It will be over too soon if I let you continue." He sat on the bed and pulled off his boots before shucking out of his shirt and standing to remove his belt. Torie's eyes never left his hands as he unbuttoned his pants and pushed them down his legs.

He stood before her, allowing her eyes to roam, inch by inch, up his body, to finally settle on his face. His nostrils flared as he caught the passion in her eyes.

"Lay back on the bed," he rasped in a ragged breath.

Jamie stretched out beside her and again began slow kisses that started at her eyes, moved down her face to her neck. He lifted his head to stare into eyes that had turned a dark violet. "I love you, Torie. You're the only woman I've ever wanted."

"Show me, Jamie. Show how much you love me," she encouraged as his dark grey eyes searched hers.

He took her face in both hands, bringing her mouth to his and took the rest of the night to show her how much he loved her.

******

"Thank you for trusting me enough to tell me the truth. The past few years I thought all I needed was the truth. Now I realize that while I wanted the truth, what I needed, have always needed, was you." He pulled her closer and kissed her hair.

It was just before dawn. They'd made love for hours and finally slept until one would wake the other to start again. Neither knew a night such as this could happen.

"Jamie?" Victoria's sleep tinged voice was soft against his skin.

"Hmm?"

"There's something else I need to tell you." Her voice waivered and Jamie could feel her tremble.

"All right." His senses went on alert. He couldn't imagine what else could be troubling her. He waited, thinking she may have fallen back to sleep.

"Hagan. He...he...," Her voice broke. She couldn't get the words to form as the pain sliced through her, remembering that day in the dirty room.

"Shssh. It's all right, sweetheart. You don't need to say any more." Jamie pulled her close and stroked her hair. "He's dead. Whatever happened is behind you, behind us. I'll listen if you want to talk about it, but nothing that he did was your fault." He hugged her tight and wished he could take away her pain.

"No, I don't ever want to talk about it. I just thought you should know everything." She took a shuddering breath.

Jamie rolled her over on top of him and touched his lips to hers for a long, lingering kiss before settling her on his chest.

She looked up into his eyes. "I do have a question."

"All right," he chuckled at the unease in her eyes.

"Who's Madeleine?"

"Ah. I figured we'd get to that. I met her a week ago. She'd just arrived and didn't know anyone. I took her to dinner last week and offered her a buggy ride to see the sights today. That's it, Torie. No more than that." He gently rolled her to her back and looked into her still sleepy eyes.

"I love you, Torie. There'll never be another. Not ever. Marry me."

Her relief was immediate. She brought her arms up around his neck, staring straight into the darkest grey eyes she'd ever seen and nodded.

"I love you too, Jamie. I've always loved you. Yes, I'll marry you."

Chapter Twenty-Four

"What are your plans today?" Jamie asked as he tucked his shirt into his pants and walked to the dresser to grab his gun belt. Strapping it on seemed so natural. The weapon had become a part of him.

She sat on the edge of the bed, watching him, entranced at his smallest action. They'd be married soon. He wanted children, lots of them, and so did she. They talked of building their home by a small creek that ran through the MacLaren ranch. He and Niall had spoken of it, but Jamie had envisioned the construction far out in the future. Now all that had changed. They'd speak to his family tonight, after meeting with her parents.

"I'm to have lunch with Mama downstairs, then shop with Gloria. Why?"

"I'd like to come by your house this afternoon, when Hen is through at the hotel. I want to ask for your hand today, not wait. I know there are still legalities with your divorce, but they shouldn't take much longer. We'll marry as soon as we can." Jamie stopped to look over at her. "If you're still sure it's what you want? To marry me?"

She laughed and ran to him, wrapping her arms around his neck and kissing each cheek before reaching up to place a soft one on his lips. "I love you too much not to marry you. This afternoon is fine. They'll be so happy for us." She stopped abruptly at a knock on the door. "I wonder who...?"

"You'd better get it. I'll step into the closet. I knew I should have snuck out earlier." He stepped inside and closed the door to the tiny space behind him.

Victoria pulled the door open only to be met by the grim features of her soon to be ex-husband. "My God, Hamilton, what are you doing here? How did you find me?" She stood firmly in place. She wouldn't let this man into her room or back into her life.

"Why, darling, where else would you be but back with your family? You're my wife and I wanted to see you. Will you not invite me in?" He tried to walk through her but she held her space and refused to budge.

"No, you may not come in, and I'm no longer your wife. At least I won't be in a few weeks. You shouldn't be here. We have nothing to say." She moved to close the door but he put a hand up, stopping the door from slamming in his face.

"I'm afraid, my dear, that those plans have changed. I think it would be best to discuss this in private. You wouldn't want the other guests to hear, would you?"

She didn't know if Jamie could hear their conversation, but felt it would be better to talk with Hamilton in the room than in front of guests in the dining parlor. At least with Jamie near, she felt safe from whatever Hamilton planned.

"All right, but only for a few minutes. I'm to meet Mother downstairs." She ushered him in and indicated one of the guest chairs. He took a seat, looking around the room before he continued.

He wasted no time stating his demands. "I don't plan to allow you a divorce, not now, not ever. I need the funds that are in your control and I won't let you take them from me. The least ugly way is for you to come home, to San Francisco, and the life we had before all these unfortunate activities occurred. You will provide me with a substantial monthly income and I will allow you a life of privacy. Of course, I'm perfectly comfortable with doing this in a less civilized fashion. As you know, I have no qualms about killing, and the first person would be your father. Your mother would be next, then Marshal MacLaren. After that, another MacLaren, then another, until you'd be left quite alone. Do you understand me, Victoria?"

She sat stunned at the extent of his brutal threats. He'd be willing to kill so many people for money. She'd known he had little character, but his threats were beyond the thoughts of any normal person.

He pulled a gun from his pocket and stood. "Now, pack your things. We're catching the stage until we can get a train. There's no point in staying in this dusty town any longer." He pointed the gun at her head and indicated the small trunk in the corner.

Jamie stood behind the door, listening to each word, deciding on his actions. He'd just made the decision to throw the door open and crush the life out of the worthless bastard when he heard Torie gasp, along with the sound of a gun being cocked. Damn, where was Wicklin? Where was Torie? He needed to know before bursting in and taking a chance that Hamilton would shoot her.

"No, Hamilton. Your threats no longer mean anything to me. You wouldn't get away with what you plan and I have no intention of going against Aunt Bea's wishes. Now, I'm staying right here, next to the bed. You leave that chair and march right out of here." To her relief, her voice sounded calm and didn't shake as she thought it would.

Good girl, Jamie thought from behind the door. She'd told him their locations, now he needed to act. He edged the door open enough to see Wicklin's gun aimed at Torie.

"Why you little bitch!" Hamilton started towards her, but then turned at the sound behind him.

"Drop it, Wicklin. Get that gun out of Torie's face or I'll shoot you where you stand." Jamie's voice brooked no argument. Any man would've been wise to heed it, but Hamilton had never been wise.

Wicklin's gun discharged. Torie screamed, looked down at the blood on her dress, and sank to the bed. Wicklin turned toward Jamie, ready to fire a second shot, when he, too, looked down to see blood flowing from his chest. It had all happened in seconds. Wicklin sank to the ground, the life already gone from his worthless body.

"Torie, no!" Jamie rushed to her. She'd fallen back onto the bed, blood soaking her dress, but she was conscious and a small smile played across her face.

"Did you kill him, Jamie?" Torie's voice was strained but calm given that Hamilton lay dead at her feet.

"Yes, sweetheart, he's gone. He'll never hurt you, or us, again." He spoke as he frantically looked her over, but only found blood on her sleeve. Hamilton had caught her in the arm, a flesh wound, nothing more. Thank God. He grabbed a pillowcase and wrapped it tight around her arm before laying her back on the bed and turning to the sound of voices in the hall.

"Who's in there? What's going on?" Jamie recognized Hen's voice.

"You'd better let Papa in Jamie. He'll just use his key anyway," Torie said as she winced in pain.

Jamie threw the door open to a crowd of ten or more, including Hen, and stood by as Torie's father took in the room, then focused on his daughter lying on the bed. He rushed to her, but she smiled, told him she'd be fine, and that Hamilton would no longer bother anyone.

Jamie watched the two, then walked to a chair, eased his shaking body into it, rubbed his face with both hands, and thanked God it was over.

Epilogue

Six months later

She bent over the basin, held her hair back, and tried to breathe. Deep, slow breaths would clear her head, or so she'd been told. At least the nausea was starting to subside. Kate had said that the first three months were the worst. After that she'd feel wonderful until about the seventh month. When she'd asked about the eighth and ninth months, Kate had just shrugged and gone to fetch a cold cloth for Victoria's forehead.

Every time Victoria looked at her stomach, softly caressed the small form growing within, she thanked God that He had finally brought Jamie and her back together. They'd married within weeks of her return to Fire Mountain and Hamilton's death. Jamie had insisted that there'd be no more waiting. Alicia, with Kate's help, had planned a beautiful wedding at the ranch with little notice.

Jamie had been resplendent in his dark pants, white shirt, red brocade vest, black tie, and black coat with tails. Her heart still raced every time she thought of their wedding day and how she'd feared it would end as if it were only a dream. But it was real, and after three months she'd told him that he'd be a father. The look on his face still brought a smile to hers.

"You ready, Torie?" Jamie called as he walked into their bedroom. He was busy building them a home of their own a mile away, in a stand of trees, overlooking a beautiful valley and creek. "Don't want to be late for this one," he said with a smile.

Sam and Gloria were to be married in a couple of hours with Jamie as the best man and Victoria as the maid of honor. Reverend Blanchard had come to Sam and Gloria when he heard of their plans, and offered to marry them. Of course, there were some conditions, but Gloria was so overwhelmed with the invitation to marry in an actual church, that Sam would have done anything the minister asked to make it happen.

They'd decided to stay in Fire Mountain so that Sam could continue doing the job he loved. The saloon sold as soon as Gloria put the word out. Ross found what he called a *silent partner* to buy the Dove, and two months ago, Gloria had officially retired. Jerrod Minton had handled the sale, representing both parties, and had firmly informed everybody that all details were sealed. They were still trying to figure out just who this silent partner was, but secrets never lasted long. It was only a matter of time.

"Just let me get this dress fastened, and I'll be ready," Torie called over her shoulder. Then firm hands covered her own and began to undo the buttons she'd already closed.

"Jamie MacLaren! What are you doing?" Torie laughed as her husband pulled her back to his chest, worked his hands inside her dress and moved them around to cup her breasts. He slowly stroked each, then let his thumbs move over each extended nipple.

"Well, maybe we have a little more time than I first thought," he whispered in her ear, kissing her neck as he worked her dress down over her hips, and let it fall to the ground. "Yes. I believe we do have all the time we want."

He proceeded to show her, in his slow, thorough way, just how much time they had.

Other books in the MacLarens of Fire Mountain series by Shirleen Davies

Tougher than the Rest

Niall MacLaren is determined to turn his ranch into the biggest cattle dynasty in the Arizona Territory. The widower will do whatever he must to obtain the political and financial support he needs, even marry a woman he does not love. Nothing will stand in his way.

Katherine is well-bred, educated, and seeks a life away from her cloistered existence in the East. Landing the teaching job in California provides her with the opportunity she seeks. Most importantly, and unlike many of her peers, she will not need a husband to achieve her goals.

When an accident brings them together, mutual desire takes root, threatening to dismantle their carefully laid plans and destroy their dreams. Can either of them afford to be distracted by the passion that unites them—especially when one of them may belong to another?

Available through Amazon, Kobo, and Barnes & Noble

Harder than the Rest
Available Fall 2013

Stronger than the Rest
Available Early 2014

About the Author

Shirleen Davies began her new series, MacLarens of Fire Mountain, with Tougher than the Rest, the story of the oldest brother, Niall MacLaren. During the day she provides consulting services to small and mid-sized businesses. But her real passion is writing emotionally charged stories of flawed people who find redemption through love and acceptance. She grew up in Southern California and now lives with her husband in a beautiful town in northern Arizona. Between them they are the proud parents of five grown sons.

Shirleen loves to hear from her readers.

Write to her at shirleen@shirleendavies.com

Visit her at www.shirleendavies.com

Thank you!

Made in the USA
Monee, IL
28 July 2021

74432190R00118